# ON THE DAY I DIED

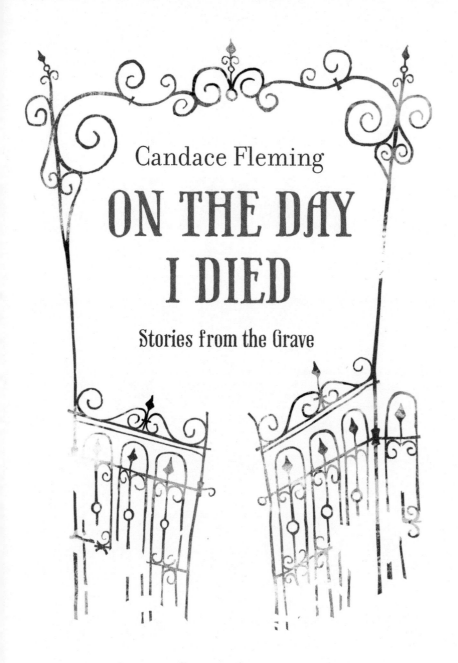

Candace Fleming

# ON THE DAY
# I DIED

## Stories from the Grave

schwartz & wade books · new york

Text copyright © 2012 by Candace Fleming
Jacket art copyright © 2012 by Jeremy Holmes

Visit us on the Web! randomhouse.com/kids

Educators and librarians, for a variety of teaching tools, visit us at randomhouse.com/teachers

*Library of Congress Cataloging-in-Publication Data*
Fleming, Candace.
On the day I died : stories from the grave / Candace Fleming.—1st ed.
v. cm.
Summary: In a lonely Illinois cemetery one cold October night, teen ghosts recount the stories of their deaths in different time periods, from 1870 to the present, to sixteen-year-old Mike, who unknowingly picked up a phantom hitchhiker.
Contents: Mike—Gina 1949–1964—Johnnie 1920–1936—Scott 1995–2012—David 1941–1956—Evelyn 1877–1893—Lily 1982–1999—Rich 1965–1981—Edgar 1853–1870—Tracy 1959–1974.
ISBN 978-0-375-86781-1 (trade) — ISBN 978-0-375-96781-8 (glb) —
ISBN 978-0-375-89863-1 (ebook)
[1. Ghosts—Fiction. 2. Cemeteries—Fiction. 3. Illinois—Fiction.] I. Title.
PZ7.F59936On 2012
[Fic]—dc23
2011018661

The text of this book is set in Filosofia and Avenir.
Book design by Becky Terhune

Printed in the United States of America

10 9 8 7 6

First Edition

For Mike and Scott, small parts of this book;
big parts of my life

# CONTENTS

Mike    1

Gina 1949–1964    14

Johnnie 1920–1936    33

Scott 1995–2012    52

David 1943–1958    63

Evelyn 1877–1893    83

Lily 1982–1999    101

Rich 1965–1981    122

Edgar 1853–1870    144

Tracy 1959–1974    164

Where the Bones Lie: A Note from the Author    193

# MIKE

It was after midnight, and Mike Kowalski was driving fast—too fast—down County Line Road. He glanced at the dashboard clock and groaned.

He was late.

Again.

His phone rang. It didn't take ESP to know it was his mother. "She probably wants to get a jump start on her griping," Mike muttered to himself.

Earlier that evening, she'd told him to be in by midnight "or else."

"Midnight?" Mike had complained. "But I'm a junior!"

His mother had rolled her eyes. "After the stunt you pulled this week, you're lucky to be allowed out at all, so I'll reiterate—midnight, or else."

Mike didn't even want to think about what "or else" meant.

Ignoring the call, he mashed down the accelerator. Maybe if he was only a *little* late . . .

That was when the girl appeared in his headlights.

One minute there was nothing but country road flanked by the thick woods of the Cook County Forest Preserve, with its one-lane bridge over Salt Creek just ahead; the next minute there she was, stumbling down the center line.

Mike slammed on the brakes. The tires squealed as the car skidded.

But the girl never flinched. Eyes wide, unblinking even in the glare of the headlights, she raised her hands palms up, pleading . . . but for what?

Mike stuck his head out the driver's-side window. The girl's skin glowed marble white, and her long, dark hair, soaked, lay plastered against her skull. Her simple cotton dress was wet, too. Mike saw water dripping from the hem. "Are you okay?" he asked.

"I'm cold." Her voice was a whisper. "I need a ride home."

Mike glanced at the clock again and grimaced. He'd rather have a root canal than experience the torture his mother was sure to have in store for him. Then again, what difference would a few more minutes make? He was already in trouble. Besides, he couldn't leave her out here alone, could he? He leaned across the front seat and opened the passenger door. "Climb in."

Wordlessly, the girl settled into the seat, and the car

filled with the smell of lavender and wet leaves. Mike watched as she slipped off her shoes—a pair of old-fashioned black-and-white saddle shoes—and neatly laid them side by side on the floor of the car. "They're brand-new," she said. Then she folded her hands in her lap and waited.

"Where to?" asked Mike. The girl's strange behavior was beginning to freak him out a little. Was she sick, or suffering from a concussion, or amnesia, or something? "Do you need a doctor?"

She pointed behind them.

Mike turned the car around, driving more slowly this time. "What's your name?"

She looked straight ahead. "Carol Anne."

"I'm Mike. Mike Kowalski." Eyes still on the road, he extended his right hand.

She didn't acknowledge the introduction, didn't even look at him.

Mike drummed his fingers on the steering wheel, curiosity getting the best of him. "So, what happened back there?"

She let several long minutes pass before answering. "I was canoeing. On Hawthorn Lake."

"After midnight? In October?"

She acted as if she hadn't heard his question. "My canoe tipped. I couldn't right it, and it was a long way to shore, too far to swim. All I could do was cling to the side and pray someone would find me. No one did."

"So how'd you finally get to shore?"

She looked at him then, and in the green glow of the dashboard she appeared even paler, her skin almost translucent in its whiteness. "The current carried me in," she answered, her voice sounding colder than the October lake. "I was in the water for a long, long time."

Mike swallowed hard. "That's awful."

"Yes," she said. Then she pointed. "Turn here."

Mike made a left onto a narrow gravel road. The car bumped along for a few miles, tree branches scratching at its paint, rocks skittering beneath its tires. It never ceased to amaze him how rural some parts of the Chicago area could be. It was like cruising through the Wisconsin wilderness or someplace.

His phone rang again.

He ignored it.

They drove deeper and deeper into the woods.

"Here," said Carol Anne at last. "Stop here."

Mike braked. In the darkness, his headlights picked out a mailbox. It read MORRISSEY. Beside it he could just make out the start of a dirt driveway.

"Is this where you live? Is that your last name? Morrissey?"

"I'll get out here," said the girl. She opened the passenger door.

"But why?" argued Mike. "It's dark. Let me drive you down to your house, make sure you get in all right."

"You know my story now," she said, climbing from the car. "But it's not the only one. There are many of us."

"What's that supposed to mean?" asked Mike.

But she had already vanished.

"Carol Anne?" he called into the darkness. "Hey, Carol Anne?"

No one answered.

Reluctantly, he headed for home.

He was already back on County Line Road when he noticed her shoes—that perfect pair of saddle shoes—sitting in a puddle on the floor mat.

Impulsively, he turned the car around and raced back toward the narrow gravel road and the even narrower dirt driveway with the mailbox marked MORRISSEY.

He found himself in front of a tired-looking farmhouse with a sagging front porch and peeling paint. In his headlights, long shadows from the surrounding trees gripped the colorless house. Every window was a dark hole, the family obviously asleep.

Maybe this wasn't such a great idea, Mike thought uneasily. Maybe I should come back in the morning.

And yet he had the oddest feeling that someone *was* awake in that old house. He knew it made little sense. The place was as silent as a grave, yet he felt that someone was there. And that that someone was waiting for him.

He got out of the car, taking the shoes with him, and mounted the porch stairs. As he raised his fist to knock, the curtain at the front window shifted. He heard a faint rustling behind the door.

He knocked.

The porch light snapped on. The door swung open. Standing there was a woman as tired and sagging as her old house. "You've come to return her shoes, haven't you?"

Mike stammered, "Y-yes, yes, how did you—"

"Someone always returns her shoes," the woman interrupted. "Always on October twenty-sixth. Every year on this very date."

"Mrs. Morrissey," said Mike, "is Carol Anne still awake? Can I speak with her, please?"

The woman gave a hollow laugh. "Carol Anne is dead, been dead fifty-six years this very night. Drowned in a canoeing accident over on Hawthorn Lake, she did. My poor baby. Her body was in that freezing water for hours."

"I . . . I don't believe you. I just saw her. I just talked with her."

"None of you ever believe me," the woman said. "But it's God's own truth. I wish it wasn't, but it is. She's dead."

Mike didn't like looking at the woman's white, sorrow-etched face. Her skin looked as if you could push a pencil through it and not draw any blood.

She went on. "Every year on the anniversary of her accident she walks County Line Road, searching, I suppose, for the help that never came. And every year she leaves her shoes. New shoes they were, bought the very morning of the accident. Oh, Carol Anne loved those black-and-white saddle shoes. To this day, I don't know why she wore them out canoeing." The woman's face seemed to collapse. "In truth, I don't know why she even went canoeing that day. It was so cold." She sniffled. "You know, I've been answering this door for decades now, reliving the horror of my baby girl's death over and over again. I'm tired of it. I can't take the grief anymore." She moved to shut the door.

"Wait!" cried Mike. "What about her shoes?"

"You want to return them to her, you'll have to take them over to the cemetery. She's buried in a special plot reserved just for young folks. I thought she'd like that, resting with people her own age."

Mrs. Morrissey pointed back the way he'd come. "You just take a right out at the gravel road, go about four miles, then take a left onto an overgrown path. The cemetery entrance is a few feet down. Look close, it's hard to spot. Not many folks go out there these days." With that, she shut the door. The porch light snapped off.

Mike made his way back to the car. His phone was ringing when he opened the door. He tossed it into the backseat. He needed to think.

He didn't know what was going on. But it couldn't be what Mrs. Morrissey claimed it was, could it? That was impossible—as impossible as an alien invasion or the existence of Bigfoot.

Yeah, if you say so, a voice whispered in his head.

But if you go home now, you'll wonder about it for the rest of your life. You'll always regret that you didn't seek out the truth.

"Forget that," Mike said aloud. Quickly, before he could change his mind, he hung a right and stepped on the accelerator.

He almost missed the dirt path. It was too narrow for the car to get down. He parked at the side of the road and, grabbing the saddle shoes, got out of the car.

From the backseat his phone went off again. Its ring sounded plaintive, beseeching.

He stopped. He should answer it. Already, he could hear his mother crying, "Oh my God, Mikey," the relief thick in her voice. "Where have you been? Come home this instant." And for the first time in his entire teenage life, he would do exactly what she said. He would turn the car around, forget about Carol Anne and her shoes and go home.

But the voice in his head whispered again, more loudly this time. It'll only take ten minutes. What's ten minutes? You're already late. And then you'll know for sure.

"Right," said Mike. He started to pick his way down the path, the sound of the ringing phone fading behind him.

The path was little more than a suggestion. He fought his way through shrubs and buckthorn, the forest pressing in from both sides. At last, what nature had worked so hard to conceal came into view.

WHITE CEMETERY. That was what the words on the metal archway read. A tall wrought-iron fence enclosed the graveyard, but the gates sagged open with age, and in places there were gaping holes where the rods had gone missing. Taking a steadying breath, Mike stepped through the gates onto consecrated ground.

The sky was bright with moonlight, although he couldn't see the moon itself; the tall trees ringing the cemetery had blotted it out. A ground mist, like vaporous tendrils, seeped from the loamy, weed-thick earth. He noticed how the path—the same one he had followed through the woods—ran like a church aisle down the center of the graveyard, ending at an algae-covered lagoon. He noticed also that nothing stirred—not the rustle of bats' wings, or the hoot of an owl, or the sigh of the rising wind. It had obviously been a long time since anyone had placed flowers or pulled weeds here.

*Forgotten.*

The word popped into Mike's head.

These graves—and the people in them—had been forgotten.

The headstones at the back of the cemetery near the lagoon looked especially old. They jutted from the earth like crooked teeth, some leaning sideways, others flat on their backs. The ones at the front were newer, and Mike bent, hands on knees, to take a closer look.

Lily
1982–1999

9

Cold droplets of mist slithered down his neck.

Seventeen, thought Mike, just a year older than me.

He felt a sudden urge to flee.

You've come this far, the voice in his head whispered. Don't you want to know if she's really here or not?

"I do," said Mike aloud, but his voice shook. All his senses were on high alert.

Warily, he worked his way through the cemetery, row by row. Most of the headstones were simple marble or granite markers, chipped or cracked by time, some crusted with lichen. Others were shaped like hearts or crosses. A few more elaborate ones showed beatific angels soaring toward Heaven with children clutched to their chests. But all of them shared one thing: the person who occupied each grave was young, somewhere between the ages of thirteen and eighteen. Fear, cold and heavy, pressed down on Mike. Now he understood what Mrs. Morrissey had meant by "people her own age."

This was a cemetery for teenagers!

He backed away, suddenly all too aware that he was alone in a graveyard in the middle of the night. His thoughts whirled, his imagination blooming. Visions of rotting corpses filled his mind. He could see their greedy fingers straining through the soil and mist, groping for one of his shoes.

In the shadowy darkness, he tripped over something, landing with a hollow thump beside a tall gravestone, roses and leaves carved deep into its granite face. Mike pushed himself to his knees and looked closer:

## Carol Anne Morrissey
### 1941–1956

He uttered a low cry as the truth struck him. He had given a ride to a ghost. But it wasn't this that sent him reeling over the edge toward terror. No, it was the realization of what he had tripped over.

Saddle shoes—fifty-five pairs of saddle shoes—lay scattered across the weed-choked mound of Carol Anne's grave. One for every year she had been dead. Some had been exposed to the weather so long that they were nothing more than strips of shapeless leather. Others were newer, covered with just a thin blush of mildew. But the newest pair—*the brand-new pair*—was the one Mike still clutched in his trembling hand.

He screamed then, flinging the shoes and shattering the tomblike silence of the graveyard.

Shhh, you'll wake the dead, the voice in his head whispered.

Too late.

The surrounding trees closed in, and the shadows deepened. The weeds tangled around his feet and ankles as if to hold him in place. Then a cloud swallowed the moon and he was enveloped in total darkness.

The wind rose suddenly, causing the tree branches to scratch and mutter.

"Listen to us. Hear us."

Breathing rapidly, as if he'd just run a long race, Mike cried, "Is someone there?"

"Listen to us. Hear us."

"Carol Anne?" he croaked. He looked around with wide, frightened eyes, his heart beating so hard he could feel it in his neck and wrists as well as his chest.

"Listen to us. Hear us."

"Go away!" he tried to scream, but he could no longer speak. His heart was hammering at a terrified pace. Collapsing onto the mound of saddle shoes, he moaned. He could see them. They were all around him. Flickering shadows as insubstantial as drawings on air— a girl wearing a long, old-fashioned skirt, a boy with a camera looped around his neck. And others. A ring of wan shapes hovering on the fringes of the shifting shadows.

It's a sign when the dead appear, the voice in his head whispered. A sign of your own death.

Mike moaned again.

"Me first." A girl moved close, and as she did, the moon reappeared, as bright and white as a polished bone. In its light, Mike could see she had on a school uniform—a cotton blouse beneath a blue plaid jumper. Around her neck she wore a string of cheap plastic pearls. She reached for Mike, her death-pale fingers trembling and eager.

"No . . . please!" Crablike, he scrambled backward over the skittering saddle shoes till his back was pressed against Carol Anne's gravestone.

The girl's hand fell to her side. "Am I as scary as

that? I don't mean to be. It's just that I've been waiting such a long time, and . . . well . . ." Her words trailed away and she looked back at the others.

"Go ahead," came a voice from the shadows.

"Tell him," urged another.

The girl turned back to Mike, and she smiled uncertainly. "We want to tell you our stories," she said. "Our *death* stories."

"Death?" rasped Mike.

She nodded, her eyes filling with luminous moonlight. "And *this* one is mine."

# GINA

## 1949–1964

JUST SO YOU GET the complete picture, I guess I should start by telling you about the Chicago neighborhood I lived in. Mine didn't have a name like Hyde Park or Roseland or Austin, but it was still a tight-knit place—what my Nonna Rosa, who came over on the boat from Italy, called *comunità*. A community.

It was the kind of place where people made Chianti in their basements and grew Roma tomatoes in the tiny yards behind their two-flats.

The kind of place where my pop—like most of the other men on our block—worked the assembly line over at the Schwinn bicycle plant, while my ma and the other neighbor ladies stayed home to do the dusting and the laundry and the daily shopping. I can still see them, those housewives, dragging their two-wheeled shopping carts along Chicago Avenue. At DiAngelo's Produce, they'd stop to squeeze the cantaloupes and complain about the price of eggplant. Next door at Mr. Santorelli's butcher shop they'd gossip and haggle over the chops, hollering stuff like "This time try giving me one that ain't all fat!"

The kind of place where kids roller-skated, and played baseball, and stayed outside until the streetlights came on, the signal that it was time to go home.

And it was the kind of place where, if you earned a certain reputation, it stuck.

Take Mrs. Gioletti, for instance. She was seventy-eight and sun-dried as a raisin, but in my neighborhood she was still "a great beauty."

Or Mr. Bianchi, who had been sober ten years but was still labeled "a stone-cold drunk."

Or me.

In my neighborhood, I would forever be known as a liar.

But I didn't tell lies. I swear.

I told stories.

They just came to me, stories about ships at sea, or long-ago murders, or how our next-door neighbor, Mr. Gamboni, was really a German spy. They weren't big stories, or mean stories. They weren't meant to hurt anyone. They were just stories with the teeniest, tiniest bits of truth buried in them. Fairy tales, really.

Like the time I turned in a report claiming that President Kennedy had come back from the dead to tell me who'd *really* shot him. You've got to admit it made a better story than sticking to the boring old facts, didn't it?

Or the time I bragged to the kids in my social studies

class, "I got a record player for Christmas," when everyone knew my pop couldn't afford to put that much under the tree. "The Beatles sent it to me themselves," I added. "There was the sweetest little note from Ringo!" It's amazing how one detail can make a story so much better.

So of course I was telling a story that March morning in 1964—the morning when everything changed.

"You won't believe who I met coming out of the library last night," I said to my cousin Annette.

We were walking to school. Annette, a few steps ahead of me, was trying to act like we weren't really together.

"Nick De Rosa." That much was true, but then I went on, "He offered to carry my books home for me. Isn't that something? Nick De Rosa, homecoming king, senior class president and Golden Gloves boxing champion, offered to carry *my* books."

Annette stopped and turned around. "Right, Gina. Yeah, I really believe that happened."

That's what Nonna Rosa calls *preso con un grano di sale*, or taking it with a grain of salt. People took everything I said with a grain of salt.

"Why can't you live in *this* world?" Annette demanded. "You know no one believes you. No one believes anything you ever say. Why do you keep making things up?"

How could I explain that my stories helped me escape the dreary sameness of my life—the same old TV shows, the same old questions from my parents, the same old mostaccioli on Thursdays and lasagna on Sundays? How could I tell her that for those few moments when I was telling the story, I slipped into a shinier world and lived the life I really wanted?

I just shrugged.

"Come on," she said with an exasperated sigh, "we're going to be late."

The sidewalks around St. Philomena swelled with kids. Patrol boys wearing those silly orange safety belts tooted their whistles and directed traffic while a couple of priests hung around the flagpole, sipping from coffee mugs and watching for fistfights.

As we passed, Father Frank waved to us. I was tempted to stop and tell him how my three-legged cat, Claudio, had saved a drowning baby, but the rush of students pushing through the front doors kept me moving. Along with the other ninth graders, I climbed the wide wooden staircase to the fourth floor.

In Sister Mary Henry's homeroom, Angela Moretti was showing off her add A Pearl necklace again. "This one," she was saying to a group of girls gathered around her, "was given to me on my last birthday, and this one was for my confirmation, and this one—"

I couldn't help myself. Tapping Angela on the shoulder, I said, "I wish I had worn *my* pearl necklace today." I didn't admit it was plastic. "*Mine* was given to me by my Nonna Rosa, not for any special occasion, but just because." I paused; then, further inspired, I added, "Actually, to be accurate, I should say it was handed down to me, since it's been in the family so long. Centuries, really. Ever since one of those old-time popes presented it to us back in the seventeen hundreds. Did you know that in Italy my family was royalty?"

Angela glared at me.

Feeling good, I took my seat.

That's when I noticed him, standing beside the blackboard—the new boy. *Pulito come una nuova spina.* That's what my Nonna Rosa would have said. "Neat as a new pin." Unlike the other boys in class, the new boy wore the white shirt of his school uniform carefully tucked into blue trousers that were creased as sharp as a razor. His necktie was knotted perfectly, and his black leather shoes shone as if he'd just rubbed them with Vaseline. He reminded me of one of those kids you'd see on the cover of *Catholic Family Magazine*—too good to be true.

He looked right at me, and I knew he'd overheard my story. Knew, too, from the way his ice-blue eyes narrowed, that he was sizing me up. Then his lips twitched into a smirky sort of smile.

Sister Mary Henry clapped her hands for attention. "Class," she said, "this is Anthony Delvecchio. Anthony comes to us from Our Lady of Mercy School."

The room buzzed. We all knew about Our Lady of Mercy. Just last week the school had mysteriously caught fire in the middle of the night. Even though only the annex had burned, it was enough to close the school and scatter its students all across the diocese.

Poor Anthony, I thought. It must be hard to lose your school.

As he took the empty desk across from me, I smiled sympathetically at him.

"Liar," he said. His voice was soft and a little contemptuous.

"Wh-wh-what?" I stammered.

"But I'm better," he added.

At the front of the room Sister Mary Henry clapped her hands again. "Gina, you know my rules about talking during class. Stand up, please."

I felt myself go hot, but before I could stand, Anthony rose.

He looked at the nun, his eyes wide and full of innocence. "I'm afraid this is my fault, Sister," he lied. "I asked . . . Gina, is it? I asked Gina to remind me of your name." He managed to blush. "I was too embarrassed to ask you myself. I mean, after all the kindness you've shown me, it felt so rude to have forgotten it." He smiled then, a single dimple appearing in his cheek. "Please forgive me, Sister. It won't happen again." He touched his hand to his chest. "I promise."

Sister Mary Henry bought every word. "Thank you for your honesty, Anthony." She practically cooed.

"*That,*" Anthony said to me as he sat back down, "is how it's done."

* * *

Anthony ignored me for the rest of the day, even though we had lunch and religion class together. I watched *him,* though. Strange, but considering this was his first day at a new school, he didn't look nervous or confused. Not the teensy-weensiest little bit. In the hall between classes, he whistled at Angela Moretti, and in the cafeteria he went right up to Nick De Rosa and thumped him on the back like they were old friends. He even shook Father Frank's hand the way my pop always did on Sundays after Mass—two-handed and full of gusto. What kind of teenager did that?

He's smooth, I thought. Smooth as the satin trim on my confirmation dress.

After school, I headed across the street to Mrs. Kostelnic's store for my daily sugar fix—acne be darned. As I stood in front of the candy counter, deciding whether to blow my entire ten cents on a Hershey's bar or just buy a nickel's worth of Atomic Fireballs, Anthony sidled up next to me.

"I heard a joke about you today," he said. "Want to hear it?"

"Not especially," I said.

He ignored me. "How can you tell when Gina Sparacino is lying?" He paused before delivering the punch line. "Her lips are moving." He laughed.

I studied a box of Milk Duds.

"What? Are you upset?" he asked.

I refused to answer. Snapping up the Hershey's bar *and* the Milk Duds, I stomped over to the cash register.

Beside it sat a dish full of matchbooks for the grown-ups who came in to buy cigarettes. Anthony strolled over to the dish and nonchalantly pocketed a couple of the books.

"I saw that," I said.

"Saw what?"

"You took some matches. They're right there in your jacket pocket."

"So what? They're free, aren't they?"

"But they're not for kids. I could tell Mrs. Kostelnic."

"Will she believe you?"

I hesitated.

Anthony stepped close, so close I could feel his breath on my cheek. "Don't you like the little *ploof* sound a match makes when it's lit?" he asked. His expression turned all intense. "Don't you like that whiff of sulfur?"

I looked away, trying to hide how frightened I suddenly felt.

At that moment, Mrs. Kostelnic hollered across the shop. "Can I help you kids?"

"I got what I came for," answered Anthony. He pushed out the door and was gone.

From then on, I made a point of avoiding Anthony. I refused to even glance in his direction during home-room, much less talk to him. I quit buying candy at Mrs.

Kostelnic's and instead walked home with Annette and her friends every day. I even started sitting with them at lunch, just in case Anthony got the bright idea to share sandwiches or something.

Annette wasn't exactly thrilled by my presence. "Can't you find your own friends?" she complained. But she didn't tell me to get lost. She couldn't. I was *la famiglia*—family.

As the days passed without any more Anthony incidents, I began to relax. Just like everyone else in my class, he'd forgotten all about me.

But one night, just before supper, there was a knock at our front door. I answered to find him standing there.

"What are you doing here?" I asked.

"I'm collecting for my paper route," he answered smoothly.

"You don't have a paper route."

He lifted his eyebrows. "How do you know? You never talk to me."

"And I'm not starting now." I tried to shut the door, but he stuck out his foot, stopping me.

"Wait," he said, his voice dead calm. "I have to ask you a question. Does my jacket smell like smoke?"

I shook my head, confused.

Anthony pointed across the street. "There's a fire over there. You better call the fire department."

I looked. Sure enough, black smoke billowed out of the Santuccis' garage.

"Fire!" I shrieked, dashing into the living room. "Ma! Call the fire department!"

Ma came to the door, wiping her hands on a dishrag and grumbling. "Honestly, Gina, if this is another one of your stories . . ."

Her voice trailed off at the sight of the flames now licking their way through the garage's tar-paper roof. With a squeak, she dropped the rag and made a dash for the kitchen and the telephone.

I turned back, but Anthony was gone.

A cold, hard fear was growing in the pit of my stomach, a suspicion turning into knowledge too awful to put into words. Could Anthony have started that fire?

It wasn't long before the entire neighborhood had left their suppers on the table to watch the firemen battle the flames. In the chaos, I saw Annette and Nick and . . . *Anthony!* He stood, mesmerized, the red-and-blue fire truck lights flashing eerily across his face.

It gave me a creepy feeling, the way his eyes were so wide and glassy. He looked like a cat staring at a bird.

The next afternoon during religion class, Sister Mary Eunice asked us to make a list of our sins. "A *written* list," she said.

Binders around the room snapped open as we reached for notebook paper.

"The purpose of this exercise is to examine your conscience so you will be prepared for your next confession," she continued. "Please be honest and earnest."

I was just wondering if I could spruce up my list, make a better story by throwing in a plane crash or maybe a movie star, when Anthony squeezed into the seat beside me.

"I'm here to confess my sins," he whispered. Glancing around to make sure no one else was looking, he dropped a sheet of paper onto my open binder.

In his recognizable block handwriting were written three little words: I DID IT.

Underneath was a drawing of Our Lady of Mercy School. It was being eaten alive by flames.

I thought I was actually going to scream. I put my fist in my mouth, as if to shove it back . . . and then just coughed. Dry-mouthed, I reached for his paper.

But Anthony snatched it back. "No, no, no," he said, waggling his finger. "This is between me and God." Then he folded his confession and stuck it between the pages of his Bible.

For the rest of the period I sat frozen beside him, sick with the knowledge of what he'd done, my heart and stomach crammed up into my throat. I had to tell someone. I had to tell Father Frank.

When the bell rang, I bolted for the door.

"What's your hurry, Gina?" Anthony called after me . . . *taunting* me!

Stifling a cry, I fled.

The hallway echoed with slamming lockers and kids shouting "Call you later" or "See you at baseball practice." I pushed my way toward the staircase. Annette and her friends were there, waiting for me. I shoved past them.

"What's with *you*?" Annette hollered after me.

But I kept going, fighting my way down the crowded stairs and out the front door.

Yes—thank God—Father Frank was there in his usual spot by the flagpole.

"Father!" I cried, tears of relief filling my eyes. "Father Frank!"

"What is it?" he asked. "Gina, has something happened?"

"Anthony Delvecchio did it," I blurted as a river of happy, laughing students flowed around us. "He set fire to Our Lady of Mercy." Then I launched into my story. But I hadn't gotten any further than the part about Mrs. Kostelnic's matchbooks when Father Frank stopped me.

"What is Our Lord's ninth commandment, Gina?" he asked.

What did that have to do with Anthony? I fumbled for a moment before answering, "Um . . . uh . . . 'Thou shalt not bear false witness against they neighbor.' "

"That is correct," said Father Frank. "And do you know what that commandment means, Gina? It means it is a mortal sin to tell lies. These untruths you are spreading about Anthony will result in your damnation unless you repent."

"But I'm not lying!"

"Storytelling, lying, it's the same thing," replied Father Frank. He took my hands in his. "You must ask God's forgiveness, Gina. You must confess."

"But . . . but . . ."

"Go home now," he said. "Go home and reflect on your sin."

I took a few stumbling steps. Then I stopped and pressed my palms to my flushed cheeks. Why wouldn't he believe me? Didn't he know I would never, ever make up a story about something this serious? Panic fluttered in my chest. What should I do? What should I do?

Anthony was waiting for me at the corner.

"Go away!" I pushed past him and hurried down the sidewalk.

He hurried after me.

Whirling, I cried, "Why won't you leave me alone?"

"Because," he replied calmly.

"Because why?"

"Because you're the only person I can tell without getting in trouble," he said.

I understood then. He needed an audience, someone to witness his deeds. If no one knew, then it was almost as if they had never happened. "Stay away from me!" I shouted. "Or I'll call the police!"

I ran, sobbing, all the way home.

"Gina, is that you?" Ma called as I burst through

the front door and flung myself into my bedroom. "Gina?"

"Leave me alone," I called back. "I'm fine."

Of course, I wasn't. But if I told her what was happening, she probably wouldn't believe me, either. I dropped onto the edge of my bed, gulping big mouthfuls of air. Hugging myself tightly, I rocked back and forth, back and forth, until finally, slowly, the panic left.

Still, a sense of dread remained.

Anthony wasn't in homeroom the next morning. Looking at the empty seat across from me, I should have felt relief. But I didn't. Instead, I felt itchy and on edge.

Halfway through the period, he appeared, making a big show of the Bible in his hand. "Please excuse my tardiness, Sister," he said as he slid into his chair, his face all false innocence, "but I was so busy memorizing my New Testament verses that I lost all track of time."

Sister Mary Henry nodded understandingly. In her world, Anthony Delvecchio could do no wrong.

I watched him out of the corner of my eye as he smiled at some secret thought. The dimple in his cheek deepened.

Minutes later, the classroom door began to clatter.

Curious, Tommy De Luca opened the door. "Hey, there's smoke in the hallway!" he hollered, just as a cloud of black smoke swirled into the classroom.

Sister Mary Henry hurried over to where Tommy

stood. Quickly, she slammed the door. But more smoke began seeping in through the transom.

Everyone looked nervously toward the teacher.

Everyone, that is, but me. I slowly turned to Anthony, my eyes wide with horror.

There was a moment, and then . . . he winked.

I leaped to my feet, the sudden movement knocking over my desk, just as the fire alarm went off.

Kids were scrambling now, bolting toward the class-room door, years of fire drill practice instantly forgotten as the smoke in the room grew thicker and blacker.

"Get down on your hands and knees!" shouted Sister Mary Henry. "Crawl out through the door one after another."

Everyone did as they were told. One by one they disappeared into the churning darkness of the hallway.

I raced to join them, but Anthony grabbed me. His strong arms held me back.

"Let me go!" I twisted and struggled.

"Enjoy it!" he shouted above the sounds of the fire. "Enjoy it for one more minute."

The room was growing hotter every second, the paint on the walls beginning to change from white to brown.

"Sister," I called weakly, choking and coughing.

Then the big globe lights that hung from the ceiling exploded, sending a rain of glass crashing to the floor. Anthony let go of my arm, and I fell to my knees.

His Bible.

In the chaos, it had been knocked to the floor. Now I snatched it up, held it over my head as if it could provide some sort of heavenly protection against the fire. But within seconds, its golden-edged pages began smoldering. They curled, became burning wisps that drifted to the floor. I put out my hand. The pages fell like snowflakes into my palm. So did a folded piece of paper—*Anthony's confession.* My fingers closed around it just as he grabbed my arm again, this time with less strength. He was making rasping, hacking sounds as he pulled me toward the windows. He wrestled one open, and we hung our heads out, gulping the cold, fresh air. Below us on the asphalt we could see Sister Mary Henry and our classmates. We could see the other students, too. Everyone had escaped—except us.

I looked at Anthony. There was a feverish light in his eyes, a strange smile on his lips. And even in the room's ovenlike heat, I shivered.

Suddenly, with a bright orange flash and a loud boom, the fire exploded. It crashed in at the door and burst through the walls. Then everything was on fire—desks, tables, books.

My hair began to smoke. I could feel my nylons melting to my legs.

"Climb up here!" shouted Anthony.

He half-dragged me out onto the wide window ledge. For a moment, we both perched there, looking down at the terrified faces below. Anthony reached over and took my clenched hand in his. "This is fun, isn't it?" he said, his voice raw. That's when the windows blew out, knocking us off the sill.

* * *

I don't know how long I lay there on the blacktop, unconscious. When I finally opened my eyes, I was looking up at Sister Mary Henry, my head resting in her lap. Father Frank bent over me, anointing my forehead with oil. " 'Yea, though I walk through the valley of the shadow of death, I will fear no evil . . .' "

*Evil.*

I moved my blistered lips, forced words up from my parched throat. "Anthony."

"He's alive," soothed Sister Mary Henry.

Father Frank leaned in even closer. "Why, Gina?" he asked, his kind eyes probing mine. "Why did you do it?"

"Anthony."

A look of sadness washed over Father Frank's face. "Oh, Gina," he sighed.

Slowly, my blackened fingers relaxed, revealing a folded paper, its edges burned—the paper that had fallen from Anthony's Bible.

Sister Mary Henry took the paper and opened it. " 'I did it,' " she read aloud. She gasped, and I knew she recognized Anthony's handwriting. She turned to Father Frank and whispered something in his ear. Their eyes met, then slowly grew wide with understanding . . . just as mine closed for the last time.

Gina fell silent.

And slowly, Mike returned to himself, the hazy edges of the ghost's story rolling back like fog to reveal the present. Once again, he could see the gravestones bright in the moonlight; could feel the saddle shoes, cold and wet and lumpy, beneath him. Nothing had changed—except for one thing. While Gina had told her story, the other ghosts had gathered around to listen, settling themselves onto nearby gravestones or sitting cross-legged in the grass. They were close enough now for Mike to make out their expressions—some sad, others hopeful, still others pitying, or sympathetic, or—in the case of the boy stomping toward him—angry.

Mike jerked back as the boy raised a fist.

But the ghost whirled on Gina. "So that's it? That's the end?"

"What do you mean?" she asked.

"You shoulda gotten even with that Anthony schmuck. You shoulda haunted him to his dying day."

"You know it doesn't work that way," said Gina. "Besides, I'm sure it all came right in the end."

"Came right? *You're* the only person can make it come right. If there's one thing I learned from my sixteen lousy years on earth, it's you only got yourself. Ain't nobody going to help. And I'll tell you something else—if it'd been me, I'd have haunted that slob until he was just a shivering little bunny rabbit. Yeah, I'd have reduced him to a quaking mass of tapioca pudding. I'd have gotten my revenge."

The boy turned his furious face toward Mike. "Revenge," he said in a low voice. "That's my story: how Johnnie Novotny got his revenge *and*"—he paused a second before continuing—"how revenge got him."

# JOHNNIE

## 1920–1936

IF YOU WAS TO ask me how I ended up in this cemetery, my life snuffed out like the burning end of some politician's fat stogie, I'd spit out two words—Officer Funkhouser. That meddling do-good copper practically pushed me into the funeral business. That's a fact. And . . . well . . . if I hadn't been at the undertaker's that night, I might not be in this graveyard now.

I was working over on LaSalle Street, relieving the well-to-do of some of their unneeded goods. Already, I'd slipped a greenback-thick wallet out of some rich swell's coat pocket, and I'd pinched a gold bangle off one of them high-class dames as she bustled off to do some shopping at Marshall Field's or one of those other swanky department stores down on State Street.

We were in a depression, see, but them hoity-toity slobs didn't know a thing about it. You can bet your last dollar they'd never stood in line half a morning just for a lousy ladleful of thin soup. Bet they'd never slept on a hard bench over in Grant Park, neither, using yesterday's copy of the *Daily News* for a blanket. Nope, life's miseries never touched them white-breads. But I sure did. And why not? I'm like that Robin Hood guy, taking from the rich and giving to the poor. They had so much. What was wrong with taking a little for myself, for cripes sake? I'm the poor!

So there I was, minding my own business and working the privileged crowd, when—*WHAM!* I found myself facedown in the gutter.

"That's it, Johnnie Novotny," bellowed a deep voice. "I'm taking you in."

I scrambled to my feet, fury boiling in my veins, fists raised. Nobody pushes Johnnie Novotny around, not unless they want a bloody lip. Then I saw who it was and I tamped down my anger. Plastered an innocent look on my face, too. "Whatcha do that for, Funkhouser?" I asked the beefy cop who towered over me. He was a giant dressed in a navy-blue woolen coat with big brass buttons. "You shouldn't go around pushing citizens, you know that?"

"You shouldn't have come back here, Johnnie," Funkhouser replied. "I told you last time that if I ever saw you working my beat again, I'd arrest you."

"I wasn't doing nothing, just walking down the street, that's all. Ain't a man allowed to walk down the street?"

"A man? You?" Funkhouser's broad shoulders shook with laughter.

My fingers clenched again. I was almost sixteen, wasn't I? Old enough to knock that smug grin clean off his stupid mug. And I was itching to do it, too, except I didn't fancy a month in the cooler. I turned to walk away.

"Oh, no you don't," said Funkhouser. Grabbing my arm, he held me tight as a vise. We started down the sidewalk, him pushing me ahead through the crush of pedestrians.

"Lemme go!" I shouted, twisting in his grasp.

"I'm doing you a good turn, Johnnie," said Funk-houser. "I'm going to recommend to the judge that he be lenient, send you to reform school instead of jail. It's the best thing for you, son. You'll be off the streets, getting three squares a day. And you'll be getting an education, too, going to regular school."

*School?*

Just the sound of that word made my neck hairs stand on end.

School?

I'd rather be in jail. Heck, in my world there wasn't much difference.

It was them teachers that put me off, namely one Miss Bolam. Jeez, but she was a real fossil, as musty as that ancient history she taught. Just looking at her gave me the creeps. Her dark eyes, cold like some kind of liz-ard's, darted from student to student. She always had it in for mugs like me—kids who came to class to catch up on their sleep while she droned on about mummies and vengeful gods and Phoenician burial spells.

*"Amun cahi ra lamac harrahya,"* she'd babble away in that wise-guy voice of hers. "That, ladies and gentlemen, is the Sumerian Resurrection Curse."

Or, "Many ancient cultures believed they could transfer death from one person to another simply by chanting this curse: *Ai oro ramr hvtar."*

Is it any wonder I couldn't keep my eyes open in class? And what was the point of it, anyways? How would all that gibberish help put food in my belly? Useless, I tell you.

The whole time she talked, her long, bony fingers would reach up to touch the brooch she always wore pinned to her collar. It was a weird-looking thing, gold with a big red stone, and shaped like a crescent moon. I wondered if it was worth pinching, if I could get anything for it. Rumor had it that it was a present from some long-dead lover, but I didn't believe that. Not for a minute. Nobody could love that paper bag.

I remember this one afternoon. She was up at the front of the class, blathering away and punctuating each boring word with a slap of the ruler she always liked to carry. "I could have been an archaeologist," she was saying. "As a young woman I trained with the greatest experts of our time. My specialty was Sumerian witchcraft practices, an obscure but fascinating subject."

That Kisser-upper, Charlene Shansky, asked her, "Why didn't you, then?"

"Unfortunately, I was hampered in my career by my fear of"—Miss Bolam paused and shuddered—"s-s-spiders." Her face turned as white as the bun on her head. "Thus I chose the classroom rather than temples and tombs."

Blah blah blah. Who cared? I made a big show of stretching and yawning.

Miss Bolam's cold eyes narrowed. "Am I boring you, Mr. Novotny?"

I answered by closing my eyes and making loud, sputtering snoring noises.

Miss Bolam moved down the aisle toward me. Even though my eyes were still closed, I could hear the squeak of her leather shoes, smell the dusty-thick stink of her lilac talcum powder.

Miss Bolam brought her ruler down—*SMACK!*—on the edge of my desk.

My eyes flew open. The entire class was staring at me.

"Hold out your hands," she demanded.

I felt hot and itchy all over.

"Other teachers may tolerate your disrespectful behavior," she said, "but not this one."

Behind me, Charlene Shansky sniggered.

"Your hands!" Miss Bolam demanded.

I knew there was only one way out—I had to give in, do what she wanted. It was the same as when my pop would stumble home from Mueller's Tavern whis-keyed up and in a wicked mood. All I could do was take the blows. Only this time it was her ruler instead of his fists. Swallowing my rage and humiliation like some bitter tonic, I slowly held out my hands. They were trembling.

She raised her ruler. "Are you scared?"

I looked straight at her. "Johnnie Novotny's never scared, you prune-faced old crone."

"You should be," she said. "You have no idea of the truly *terrible* punishment I could mete out if I wanted to. But for today . . . this will do."

She brought down her ruler, slicing it through the air like one of them guillotines she was always talking about. It smashed into my knuckles, bruising bones and break-ing skin. A red-hot pain shot up my arm. But I know how not to cry. I just gritted my teeth as she smacked me again . . . and again . . . and again.

When she finished, she leaned in close. "Have you learned your lesson, Mr. Novotny?"

I wasn't about to give her the satisfaction of an answer. But as she walked away, I vowed under my breath, "I'll get even with you. Just you wait."

Two days later, I left a little surprise in Miss Bolam's desk drawer—the drawer where she kept that ruler.

"Did everyone do their homework?" she asked as she came striding into the room. Her black eyes landed on me.

I smiled at her, all sweet and innocent-like.

Her fingers reached up to briefly touch her brooch; then she pulled open the drawer.

Spiders—a wave of twitching black and brown legs—poured out. They scurried between Miss Bolam's fingers and scampered up her arms. They dropped to the floor and crawled across her shoes. An especially furry house spider hopped onto her crepe-skinned cheek. And a daddy longlegs caught its breath on the red stone of her brooch before slipping down the neck of her blouse.

I leaned forward. I couldn't wait to hear the old bat scream.

But Miss Bolam didn't scream. Instead, she froze. Her black eyes bulged and her dried-apple face turned the color of oatmeal. A choking, gargling noise rose from deep in her throat, and then . . . she just dropped into a heap on the floor.

A big gray spider darted across her shoe.

Carol-Marie Price screamed and Charlie Groth ran to get help. An ambulance came and took Miss Bolam away. She never came back to school. We heard later that she'd had a stroke and was tottering at death's door.

But that wasn't my problem. She'd asked for it, right?

No, my problem turned out to be Charlene Shansky. Seems Charlene had seen me pull that spider-filled Mason jar out of my knapsack, and as soon as the ambulance carrying Miss Bolam took off, she hightailed it for the principal's office. An hour later, I was sitting across from Mr. Davenport.

I tried to put on my innocent look. I told him it was just a prank, a practical joke that had gotten a little out of hand. But Mr. Davenport didn't have a sense of humor.

"I have no choice but to expel you," he said.

My fists balled. I tell you, I came close to breaking the guy's nose. But then I thought, Who cares? I'm sprung! It wasn't like I loved learning or anything like that. The only reason I ever went to school was to get away from the old man.

"You just done me a favor," I told the principal. Head high, I sauntered out.

I kept walking, too, all the way to Grant Park, where a couple of guys I knew from the neighborhood were living. I didn't go home. What was the point? Pop would have just slapped me around for getting kicked out of school. No, I decided, I was a free man, and now I needed to make my own living.

And school?

Well, that just wasn't part of the plan.

"Take that, Funkhouser!" I shouted at the cop. Using all my strength, I flung my head back, slamming it into his blocky chin. His regulation square-brimmed cap fell to the sidewalk and his lip gushed blood. He raised his hand to his mouth, loosening his grip on me for a second. I twisted away and vaulted into the busy street.

"Johnnie, come back!" shouted Funkhouser. But he didn't chase after me. He just stood on the curb and watched as I dodged around delivery trucks, sedans and cranky old Model Ts.

I looked back over my shoulder and raised my hand in salute to him. "So long, sucker!" I cried.

There came a horn blast and a squeal of tires as a hearse braked to a stop just inches away from me.

"Jeez, kid," said the driver, sticking his head out the window. "You came close to being my next customer."

I looked at the hearse—a Packard, it was, long and black and sleek. Through its windows I could see the ornate silver handles of the casket shimmering against dark wood like some hidden treasure. Jeez, that stiff had more dead than I'd ever had alive.

And that's when it came to me, just like that. Why bother pinching stuff off living people when there were so many *dead* people lying around? Dead people still had stuff—rings and watches and whatnot—but they couldn't yell for help or call the cops. You don't get sent to reform school for stealing a corpse's pocket watch (or at least, I didn't think you did). And it would be easy—as easy as taking candy from . . . well . . . a *dead* baby.

I started laughing right there in the street, the hearse driver staring at me as if I'd lost my marbles. "Thanks, Funkhouser," I said aloud. "Thanks a million."

Back in those days, Chicago was lousy with funeral homes, what with all them gangsters running around, drumming up business. Honest, a guy couldn't cross the street without stumbling onto one of them death joints.

They was on practically every corner. Most of the under-takers ran their businesses out of their own homes. Down in their basements was where all the body work took place—draining the blood, pumping the bodies full of the stuff that kept them from looking like overheated nectarines, dolling them up with makeup and dressing them up in their Sunday best.

The main floor was where they displayed the bodies. They had these big, long rooms they called parlors that were all decked out with curtains that looked like those fancy dresses the nobs' wives wore to their stupid music shows down on West Monroe. And there was heavy wood furniture and thick carpets, and pictures of Jesus and bronze crosses on the walls. Sometimes—in the fancier joints—there'd even be a stained-glass window or two. The casket always sat on a bier, a sort of table, at the front of the parlor, sometimes in its own little nook.

Upstairs, right on top of all this dead-body stuff, was where the undertaker and his family lived. At first I wondered what it was like to go to bed every night know-ing there was a corpse laying right downstairs. But then I'd seen stiffs before, and they didn't move. Dead and gone, right? Besides, I figured this was normal for them, just like sleeping in the park was normal for me. People get used to their own lives, you know?

I'll tell you one thing about funeral homes, though. They were easy pickings. All I had to do was wait until the middle of the night, when I was sure the undertaker and his family were fast asleep, then open a window and creep right in. The windows in those places were never locked, which seemed downright stupid to me. But, then, who was I to look a gift horse in the mouth? Those undertakers' trusting natures just made my job that much easier.

Once inside, I'd ease open the big double door that led into the parlor. Then I'd slip along through the shadows—those thick carpets conveniently muffling the sound of my footsteps—until I came to the casket.

Opening a casket's lid was like opening a box on Christmas morning—you never knew what you'd find inside. A pocket watch? A gold wedding band? A set of pearl cuff links? Eagerly, I'd slide my nimble fingers under the rim of the lid until I found the release tab. The lid would open with a sigh, the stiff would come into view. Always polite, I'd introduce myself.

"Excuse me, ma'am," I'd say as I slipped off her ring. "The name's Johnnie."

Or other times,

"Thank you kindly, sir," as I unsnapped a tie pin.

Or once in a while,

"Sorry, kid," as I pocketed a baseball card or a Shirley Temple doll.

Business was booming! As long as people kept dying, I was in clover.

Then one night I slipped into the Swickard Funeral Home over on Ashland and Grand. It was smaller than the other joints I'd robbed—just one tiny parlor that stunk of cooked cabbage and mothballs. Wooden chairs— the flimsy, folding kind—had already been set up for the next day's funeral, and even in the dark I could see that the carpet was thin-to-none in spots.

Johnnie, I told myself, as sure as eggs is eggs, you won't be walking out of *here* with no diamond necklace. Still, even a poor corpse might have a bauble or two. Creeping easy, I moved toward the front of the parlor where the cheap pine coffin lay.

And then I stopped. It was a humid June night, and the block of ice that had been placed under the bier to keep the body cool had created a fog bank of pale vapor that swirled, ghostlike, in the parlor's dim light. I tell you, it gave me a creepy feeling, as if I was stumbling onto the set of one of them Wolf Man movies. I paused, got a grip.

Reaching the casket, I placed my hands on the lid and took a deep breath. Then, quiet, all cautious-like, I raised it, inch by inch, the thrill starting to build inside me as the contents of the coffin came into view.

"Come on," I muttered, my voice sounding like it did when I was shooting dice, "make it a wedding band, a silver cross, a pair of gold earrings."

Hopes high, I leaned in through that weird fog and— leaped back, knocking over one of them folding chairs. The clatter echoed in the empty room.

For a couple of seconds I was glued to the spot,

bent over, my heart *rat-tat-tat*ting in my chest like a Tommy gun.

It couldn't be!

But it was!

The face—them waxy, bloodless features—belonged to none other than . . .

Miss Bolam!

I swallowed hard, my throat feeling all thick and woolly. I'm not afraid, I told myself. It was just creepy, seeing someone dead that I'd seen alive only a few weeks earlier.

I straightened and forced myself to look in. There she lay, her cobweb-white hair done up in her everyday bun, her skin wrinkled as a mummy's. Her eyes were closed, sure, but in my mind I could see them lifeless black marbles beneath the lids.

A glint of something pulled my eyes away from her face. Pinned to the collar of her death dress, Miss Bolam's brooch glittered in the mist.

My lips, which had been pressed together so tightly they ached, suddenly relaxed into a smile. Poetic justice. That's what it was, all right. Poetic justice. Miss Bolam's precious brooch was about to buy me pecan pie over at Alma's Diner for the next year!

I reached for it.

And then, by some crazy trick of light, one of Miss Bolam's yellow, melted-looking hands seemed to move. Except it wasn't a trick of light, because . . . the hand moved again. Twitched. Lifted off her chest. Then it slid down, inch by inch, its long nails making a scratching sound as they dragged across the casket's satin lining until it finally came to rest at her side.

I pulled away. Squeezed my eyes shut. Opened them again.

Come on, Johnnie. Get a grip. It's just some kind of dead-person reflex, the body settling or something. You're spooked and letting your mind play tricks. What with the fog, and finding your old teacher like this, you're imagining things.

I made myself reach down again, my fingers feeling thick as sausages, and unpinned the brooch. The metal felt cold in my hand. As cold as that block of ice sitting under the bier.

Time to skedaddle, I told myself. Yeah, hightail it out of here *now*. Letting the coffin lid fall shut with a dull thump, I turned and made my way through the rows of cheap chairs. I was already at the double doors, already turning the knob, when I remembered. *Her hand.* Tomorrow morning when the undertaker opened the coffin, he'd see that Miss Bolam's hand wasn't crossed over her chest anymore. He'd take a closer look, discover that the brooch was gone and squawk to the cops. Sure as beans on toast, by tomorrow night there'd be nothing in the papers and on the radio but news about the funeral home robbery. And my perfectly good business? So long and good night! Everything spoiled because of dusty Miss Bolam.

I shook my head. That dame had been in the driver's seat while she was alive. I wasn't about to let her run things when she was dead, too.

I made myself turn around, forced one foot in front of the other. Drops of sweat the size of dimes clung to my forehead, and my breath came in whistly gasps, like a Model T that's split an air hose. Hands shaking, I opened the coffin's lid for a second time.

"Miss Bolam?" I whispered crazily.

She lay there, cold and stiff. Unmoving.

I took a step backward. I didn't want to get anywhere near her.

Do it, Johnnie. Just do it, and get outta here.

I stretched out my arm. Wispy fingers of fog reached into the casket along with me. My belly clenched as I grasped her dead hand.

It grasped back.

I screamed. Scrambling backward, I tried to pull away, but the hand held on like a vise, the dead fingers digging into my flesh. In its coffin, Miss Bolam's body was dragged onto its side. Its mouth fell open, gaping. One eyelid, like a broken window blind, rolled halfway up. With a final frantic tug, I flung the hand off. It fell back against the side of the coffin with a sickening thunk.

I screamed again, sucking in lungfuls of that yellowish coffin fog. I whirled, and in my fear fell head-over-hobnails into the front row of folding chairs. I went down, the chairs toppling onto me. I kicked them away. Struggling to my feet, I glanced back at the casket.

Everything was the way it had been before!

The body lay on its back, mouth and both eyes closed, hands crossed over its chest. The only thing different was the brooch. It no longer gleamed from Miss Bolam's collar. It was mine now, stuffed into my shirt pocket, cold against my chest.

I couldn't have dreamed this all up, could I? I had screamed, for cripes sake. I had tripped. I had seen that hand move.

But if it wasn't my mind playing tricks, why hadn't the undertaker burst in? Surely he'd heard all the racket.

My brain felt fuzzy and confused.

I looked back at Miss Bolam's corpse.

"Dead and gone," I said aloud.

At that, the fog thickened and swirled, and the parlor's curtains billowed as if there was a breeze blowing somewhere, which there wasn't because the windows were closed tight. Behind me, the parlor doors squeaked shut.

I lunged for the doorknobs, turned, pushed. The doors wouldn't budge. It was as if someone—or something—was holding them from the other side, refusing to let me out.

In my pocket, that brooch suddenly started throbbing . . . no . . . beating, beating like a human heart. And where it had once been icy, it now burned through my shirt. I could feel the red stone in its center glowing.

Then a voice spoke from behind me—Miss Bolam's

voice—sounding like dry leaves on a sidewalk and spouting words I didn't understand. *"Amun cahi ra lamac harrahya."*

I turned slowly.

Miss Bolam was sitting up in her casket. Her head slowly swiveled until she was facing me. She looked deep into my eyes with her flat, dead ones. Then her lips parted like an open wound, and out crawled a single black spider.

My knees buckled. With a shriek, I pounded, kicked, flung myself against the doors. I cast a frantic glance over my shoulder.

Miss Bolam was out of her casket now. She staggered toward me, her leather shoes squeaking. *"Amun cahi ra lamac harrahya."*

I whimpered and shook the doorknobs.

She kept coming, step after squeaking step. Trapped like a rat, I could only watch, my back pressed against the doors, as she moved closer and closer, until finally she stood close enough for me to feel the chill rising off her dead flesh. Her dried-apple face pressed against mine.

*"Ai oro ramr hvtar."*

I heard a new voice. A man's voice. The undertaker's voice!

"You're a fine lady, Miss Bolam," the undertaker was saying, "to pay for all the boy's funeral expenses. A former student of yours, did you say?"

"Yes." It was Miss Bolam's voice again, but this time she didn't sound like dead leaves. This time she was using her old classroom voice. "It's such a shame. Johnnie had such promise."

"I'm alive!" I tried to yell. But my lips wouldn't move. Nothing would move. I could only lie there, stiff as stone.

The dusty-thick stink of lilac talcum powder filled my nose; then Miss Bolam's face came into view. She was fully alive now and grinning with triumph. Leaning over to pin the brooch onto the collar of my dress shirt—the light in its center starting to fade—she whispered in my ear, "We all learn our lesson, Mr. Novotny, one way or the other."

The coffin lid closed with a creak.

Mike watched as Johnnie, no longer angry, yanked the brooch off his collar. "It don't look like much now, does it?" he said. His voice sounded both hurt and bewildered.

Mike looked at the brooch. Tarnished gold. A dull red stone. He shook his head. Above them, the wind sighed through the trees.

Finally Gina said, "Did you try to haunt her? Miss Bolam, I mean. Did you get your revenge?"

"I thought about it," said Johnnie, tucking the brooch into his trouser pocket. "And I woulda done it too, but then . . . well . . . I sort of figured I had it coming, what with the spiders and all."

"Poetic justice," Mike whispered to himself.

Johnnie heard him. "Yeah, that's right," he said. "Poetic justice."

"That's crap," said a new voice. The boy with the camera hopped down from a weather-stained statue of an angel. "If you want to think you got what you deserved—somehow earned your fate—then go ahead. But there's no way *I'm* buying that poetic justice baloney. *I* didn't deserve my fate. I didn't have it coming. It just happened. Death's like that, you know? Capricious." He paused, then laughed, a deep, rich laugh. "How's that for an SAT vocab word, huh? *Capricious.*" He pointed. "Hey . . . um . . . what's your name?"

"Mike."

"Hey, Mike, you want to hear a capricious story?"

Do I have a choice? thought Mike.

# SCOTT

## 1995–2012

THE CHICAGO STATE ASYLUM for the Insane—or what was left of it, anyway—was just six blocks from my house. The place had been abandoned so long even my dad couldn't remember a time when it was open, and he'd lived in the neighborhood his entire life—almost fifty years! Left to decay, it was creepy as crap. Its gables and towers jutted into the stormy sky like evil fists, and its dark windows made me think of a skeleton's eye sockets. You know, bleak and empty, but still full of secrets. Its paint peeled. Slates from its roof littered the overgrown ground. And you could hear rusting KEEP OUT signs banging whenever the wind howled.

Oh, yeah, Dracula would have loved this place.

So would Edgar Allan Poe.

And me. Most definitely me. Already, I could imagine a series of my black-and-white photographs of the place hanging on the art room wall; already hear Mr. Adair, the honors art teacher, saying something like "Forlorn and intriguing, exuding a sense of transience, the ruins of the asylum are a reminder of mortality, proof that nothing is forever."

A+ work for sure. I'd probably even score a primo spot in the senior exhibition. And why not? A project like this would be *epic*!

The idea had come to me the night my buddy, Aidan, and I were hanging out in his basement stuffing our faces with leftover Chinese and flipping through the cable channels. Aidan tucked a forkful of lo mein noodles into his mouth, then came to a total stop.

"Cool," he said, noodles dangling, "*Specter Searchers*!" He dropped the remote and reached for the soy sauce.

We watched as a couple of so-called paranormal experts—a big-gutted guy with a face full of piercings, and a girl who could definitely have used a couple of doughnuts—stumbled around a dark basement.

"Oooh, did you see that?" gasped the girl, whirling and shining her flashlight into a corner littered with crushed beer cans and cigarette butts.

"It was a ghost," declared Gut Guy, as if his saying so made it true.

The girl rubbed her bony arms. "It's cold," she whimpered.

"A cold spot," said Gut Guy. Then, for those viewers who still might not have connected the dots, he added, "A cold spot is an indicator of paranormal activity."

I couldn't stand it. "This is all a crock," I erupted. "There aren't any ghosts down there."

"They just found one, didn't they?" Aidan said, pointing at the screen with a cold egg roll.

"They *said* they found one. But where's the proof— the irrefutable, scientific proof?"

Aidan stared at me blankly. Let's face it. He wasn't exactly a brainiac. Still, he had other things going for him. Like his laid-back personality. Like the fact that he could put up with what some of the other kids at school called my superiority complex.

What? I'm supposed to apologize for being smart?

"Who needs proof?" Aidan finally said with a shrug. "Ghosts just *are*."

And that was when it struck me—I'd do a little urban exploration of my own! But instead of stumbling around in dark corridors and moldy basements looking for ghosts, I'd set out to prove that there was no such thing. That ghosts were merely the result of superstitious minds and tiny intellects. Urban legends created by people willing and eager to believe the unbelievable. And I knew just where I'd go—the Chicago State Asylum for the Insane.

"You're kidding, right?" said Aidan after I told him my idea. "That place rates like a two hundred on the haunt-o-meter!"

I knew the stories, of course. Everyone in my neighborhood knew them. Stories of flickering lights; of crazed, disembodied laughter and shrieking; of the occasional trespasser seeing moving shadows and floating orbs.

"It's all crap, Aidan," I said. "Come with me and I'll prove it to you."

"No way am I going poking around in there. And you shouldn't either. Annabelle might get you."

"Annabelle?"

"You mean to tell me you haven't heard about *Annabelle*?" He leaned forward, pushing aside a half-empty carton of mu shu pork. "A few years ago some guys were in there, drinking beer and goofing around, when they hear this giggling sound coming from the third floor. So they go upstairs and they see this little girl sitting next to the barred window in this old-fashioned-type wheelchair. Her hands and legs are all bound up with leather straps, you know? And when she turns to face them they realize . . . she doesn't have any eyes! 'My name is Annabelle,' the little girl says, all whispery. 'Want to play a game? I know some fun games.' And she smiles this crazy warped smile. But no way are those guys sticking around to play Ring Around the Rosy with a dead kid. They race for the door. 'Don't leave me!' the little girl cries after them. 'Don't leave me!' Later, those guys swore they felt Annabelle holding them back with, like, some kind of supernatural power or something." He paused. "I'm telling you, Scott, those dudes were lucky to escape."

"Those dudes were dipsticks," I said.

"Whatever," said Aidan. He burped. Changed over to the sci-fi channel.

Aidan's bogus story didn't stop me, of course. I was already on fire with the idea's possibilities, already basking in the glory I knew I'd earn.

I raised the viewfinder of my Canon EOS 30D, framed and snapped. As I did, a spiral of dust and dead leaves whirled up the ruined circular driveway toward me. Black clouds darkened the already gloomy building. Lightning forked and thunder rumbled. Time to go inside.

Ignoring a NO TRESPASSING sign that had been up so long its post was almost completely rotted through, I shouldered my camera bag and squeezed under the buckling chain-link fence. I raced up the driveway, taking the asylum's crumbling stone stairs two at a time. But before diving for cover inside, I paused for a closer look at the arch above the front door. Carved into the lichen-spotted granite were the words ABANDON ALL HOPE YE WHO ENTER HERE.

I recognized the quote. It was the inscription at the entrance to Hell from Dante's *Divine Comedy*. I had to grin. Who would have thought I'd actually use something I learned in AP English?

Stoked, I snapped a couple of pictures, then glanced farther upward. Something was there, watching me. A face. Peeking out from beneath the eaves. I froze, then relaxed. It was just a gargoyle, the icy, unsettling face of a gargoyle. Its fanged mouth gaped open in a malevolent grin, its wicked eyes bulging with rage.

Awesome.

Mindless of the strengthening wind that tugged at me, I clicked off some shots. I could almost hear Mr. Adair saying, "That's one for your college portfolio, Scott. The admissions officers at the Art Institute are going to love it."

After I left Aidan's that night, I went home and did a little online research. And let me tell you, Chicago State Asylum had a crazy history—no pun intended:

Fact #1: In 1851, Cook County thought the still-rural northwest side of the city would be the perfect place for an insane asylum. So the county bought forty acres of farmland, built a creepy hospital that looked like a castle and started packing in the crazies. It was easy to do. Back in the day, lots of people—especially women and children—were declared insane when the county didn't know what else to do with them. Eventually the place became a dump for orphans, unwed mothers, kids with Down syndrome or autism, sick war vets, old folks and lots of other people society cast off.

Fact #2: By the 1880s the place had more than two thousand patients crowded onto its three floors. With that many people, living conditions were bound to suck. Chicago State was notorious for bleeding, freezing and shackling its patients. Ghostlike inmates wandered aimlessly through the wards. They went without clothes, starving and sleeping in filth-strewn hallways. And still, every day more and more patients arrived. Most came by railway, in a specially built car complete with chains and leather restraints, known around those parts as the crazy train.

Fact #3: Chicago State was constantly making headlines. My favorites? PATIENT BOILED TO DEATH IN BATHTUB; CHILD IMPALED ON HOSPITAL FENCE WHILE TRYING TO ESCAPE; or best of all—HOSPITAL'S BEAUTY PARLOR CLOSED AFTER HEADLESS BODY FOUND.

I planned on using the headlines as captions for my photographs. See? I told you so . . . epic!

Thunder crashed even louder than before, and lightning forked across the asylum's steeply pitched roof, leaping from tower to tower like a special effect in a Frankenstein movie. The sky had turned into an ugly purple bruise. Raindrops, cold and hard as marbles, pelted my back, soaking my T-shirt. Clicking off one last shot of the gargoyle, I pushed open the heavy door and plunged into the asylum's main hall.

Inside, the darkness was total, as if the place was holding blackness within itself. As I stood there, catching my breath and hoping my eyes would adjust, the door behind me swung shut. A deathly cold crept down the bleak corridors, wrapping itself around me. From deep inside the asylum came the sound of something like iron doors clanking against their frames.

I lifted my camera and took a few careful steps forward.

Lightning flashed, illuminating the place in both darkness *and* whiteness, like a photograph—one of *my* photographs. In that instant I made out fallen plaster and peeling walls. An old-fashioned cane-back wheel-chair sat at the foot of a narrow staircase. Then all went black again, and stupid as it sounds, I had the weird feeling that someone was watching me.

"Like who, Annabelle?" I said aloud just so I could hear my own voice.

My words echoed in the darkness. I touched the camera hanging around my neck. Reassurance. A reminder of why I was there.

Outside, lightning flashed again, brightening the room.

Was it my imagination, or . . . had that wheelchair moved?

I took another tentative step, my knees weak.

It's funny how your imagination can work on you: forcing your mind down paths your logical self would never have taken; filling your head with thoughts you know are crazy. Thoughts like—Did I just hear a footstep upstairs? Or, Who is that standing in that corner? Even if there are no ghosts, the mind creates them.

More lightning.

Another cautious step.

A moaning squeak, like a rusted wheel turning, whispered somewhere in the room. A high-pitched laugh gurgled down the staircase. I felt something moving—just *barely* moving—around me. The wind?

I stopped.

*What are you, an idiot, or something? You saw the TV show. You heard the stories. Are you really going to explore a supposedly haunted asylum all by yourself in the middle of a thunderstorm?*

NO WAY!

Whirling, I ran back to the door, grasped the knob, pulled.

"Bye-bye, Annabelle!" I shouted.

The door opened without resistance. Why was I surprised? Had I expected something else?

I paused beneath the arch of the doorway and took a deep breath. Outside, a curtain of rain bowed the trees and flooded the streets. Thunder growled across the storm-tossed sky. But that didn't stop me. Senior exhibition or no senior exhibition, no way was I going back inside. Tucking my camera under my shirt to protect it from the downpour, I stepped away from the Chicago State Asylum for the Insane.

There was an explosion of thunder. A skull-clutching crack. Like a strobe at a nightclub, lightning flashed. And flashed. And flashed again. Above me, the gargoyle tipped, rocked, seemed to lean from the eaves. Then its grinning face fell . . . no, *leaped* at me.

Pain sliced through my head. I crumpled, my blood mingling with the rainwater, turning the puddles red. Beside me, the gargoyle lay with a stony smirk. I heard gurgling laughter, the sound of a squeaking wheel. "Don't leave me." Then, from beneath my twitching body, I felt my camera click.

My final photograph.

Overhead, the moon cleared the trees, creating a white circle of light directly in front of Carol Anne's grave.

It's like a spotlight, thought Mike, like a spotlight on a stage. In it, he could see the camera's bent frame, its smashed lens.

"I'm sorry," he said at last, wishing he could think of something—*anything*—better to say. After all, it had to be painful reliving your own death.

Scott shrugged. "Yeah . . . well . . ."

"Sorry?" exclaimed Johnnie with a snort. "It's hilarious! Clocked by a stone gargoyle! Who woulda believed it?"

"Me." A kid sporting a crew cut moved into the circle of light. "After what happened to me, I'd believe anything." He cleared his throat, waited until everyone was looking at him before continuing. "Have you ever seen that movie *The Blob,* or maybe *Attack of the Crab Monsters*? I bet you thought they were pure fiction, right, Mike?"

"Aren't they?" asked Mike.

"Nope," said the kid. "Those movies were based on *fact,* and the truth is that when I was alive, aliens from outer space were crashing in the New Mexican desert; radiation was seeping into everyone's water, creating mutant creatures; and in my town of Rolling Meadows, Illinois, something stranger than any movie happened. I swear."

# DAVID

## 1943–1958

"I'VE SAVED A WHOLE dollar," my kid sister, Toni, said on that fateful August day. She was perched on one of our pink kitchen countertops, licking pimento cheese off a celery stick and scanning the advertisements at the back of her *Crypt of Terror* comic book. "Now all I have to do is decide what to buy."

"Save your money," I replied. "All that stuff is junk."

"Junk?" squealed Toni. "Are you kidding?" She started to read. "'Hypno-Coin! Amaze your friends with fascinating hypnotic tricks of memory and mezmerization.'" She giggled. "Wouldn't that be swell at Lori Beth's next sleepover?"

In answer, I rolled my eyes and took a bite of my own celery.

Toni read on. "'Defend the future with your very own Captain Gizmo Atomic Ray Gun. Use the patented destructive sparking action to foil Martians and monsters.' "

I snorted. "Yeah, *that's* real."

She looked up from her magazine. "When did you turn into such a sour-faced old grandpa?"

"Since I got stuck babysitting you."

*"Waaaa!"* She rubbed her eyes, pretending to cry. "Poor Davey-wavey has to stay home with me instead of making time with Barbara Petersen over at Moe's Drive-In. *Waaaa!*"

I felt my temper rise. Why, I asked myself for the umpteenth time, did Mom and Dad's wedding anniversary have to be *this* weekend? And why did they have to take off in Dad's brand-new Bel Air for some fancy resort in Michigan? Couldn't they have just gone out to dinner like other parents?

I narrowed my eyes at my sister. "You're a brat."

"Sticks and stones," she said. She stuck out her tongue, then went back to reading. "Onion-flavored gum . . . shrunken heads . . . Insta-Pets." She paused, and I could see her lips moving as she read the ad to herself. Then she looked up, her dark eyes twinkling with excitement. "Listen to this! 'Enter the amazing world of man-made life with Insta-Pets—the real, live pets you grow yourself. Fun and fascinating. Just add water.' "

"Like what? Insta-poodles? Insta-hamsters?" I laughed mean-spiritedly.

"Well, I saved up my allowance, and I'm going to find out," said Toni. Hopping off the counter, she picked up her magazine and pushed through the swinging kitchen door.

"It's a stupid waste of money," I called after her.

Her bedroom door slammed.

Early the next morning, just as the sun was rising, the doorbell rang. Still sleepy-eyed and wearing my pajamas, I answered. A bright red box sat on the stoop. It was addressed to Antoinette Turlo.

"They're here! They're here!" Slipping past me, she swooped up the box.

"What's here?" I asked. "What is that?"

"My Insta-Pets," she replied. "I ordered them yesterday."

I shook my head. "That's impossible. There's no way they could have gotten here so quickly."

Toni shrugged and held up the box. "But they did! See?"

She tapped the package's return address.

INSTA-PETS
A DIVISION OF GALACTIC OOZE TOYS

"How'd that package get to us overnight?" I asked. "And who delivered it?"

Toni shrugged again. "Who cares? All that matters

is it's here! It's here!" She danced off to the kitchen, the red box clutched to her chest.

Perplexed, I stepped out onto the front porch and looked up and down our wide, tree-lined street. Everything looked normal—lawn sprinklers and station wagons and pastel ranch houses standing neatly in a row. A whiff of burning charcoal from last night's barbecue grills still hung on the morning air. It mingled with the scent of fresh-mown grass and well-tended flower beds, becoming what Mom liked to call "the sweet smell of the suburbs."

A summer calm laid its hand over me. I spied Mr. Kopecky bringing in his newspaper, and Mrs. Neary taking Muffin, her nasty-tempered Pekingese, out for a walk. It all seemed like a typically cheerful, unchangingly bright morning in Rolling Meadows, except . . . there wasn't any sign of a mailman. No sign of a delivery truck, either.

Strange.

I walked back into the house.

In the kitchen, Toni had already torn open the package and was laying out an assortment of foil envelopes on the Formica table. Each had a picture of a smiling creature with three horns, scales and a forked tail. The girl creatures had big red bows in their horns. The boys wore cowboy boots.

"See, David?" said Toni. She handed me the first of the envelopes, labeled INSTA-PET EGGS. "All I have to do is follow the directions and poof—Insta-Pets!"

I riffled through the other envelopes. They had names like SASSY FEAST PET CHOW and INSTA-TREATS AND SWEETS.

Toni had already measured water into Mom's crystal punch bowl and was now adding something labeled INSTA-PET WATER PURIFIER. It smelled like dirty feet.

Idly, I wondered if the neighborhood ladies would notice a weird taste the next time Mom served punch at one of her card parties. I imagined Mrs. Neary taking a sip, then coughing, choking and pounding on her twin-set and pearls before finally managing to sputter, "Betty, dear, did you clip this recipe from *Good Housekeeping*?"

I snorted at the thought.

"Quit daydreaming and do something, will you?" said Toni, who was now up to her elbows in measuring cups and foil envelopes. She handed me the instruction sheet. "Here, read that to me."

I peered at the tiny print. "Did you add the purifier to exactly sixteen cups of water?" I asked.

"Yeah, yeah, I already did that," she replied. "What's next?"

"Um . . . uh . . . add both the Grow Kwikley Growth Stimulator and the Plasma III to the purified water and stir. Add eggs."

Toni pawed through the envelopes until she found the right ones. Tearing open the growth stimulator, she sprinkled its powdered contents into the water. Then from a thick silver envelope marked PLASMA III, she began squeezing out a mysterious-looking green sludge.

" 'Warning,' " I said, still reading the instructions. " 'DO NOT ADD ANY INGREDIENTS BUT OFFICIAL INSTA-PETS PRODUCTS TO YOUR PETS' WATER.' "

Toni stirred the ingredients together with a wooden spoon. It turned green.

"Yum, breakfast," I said.

She ripped open the egg envelope. "Here goes nothing." Two ordinary-looking, quarter-sized discs plopped into the water.

Instantly, a silvery mist rose from the punch bowl and the water turned deep blue. The mist began to spin crazily like that teacup ride at Disneyland, spiraling higher and higher till it finally twirled into a mini-cyclone that churned and spewed across the water's surface.

"Wow!" gasped Toni.

Mom's punch bowl began to look eerily like a little ocean, with miniature whitecaps rolling and tossing and sending up spume. Then, just as fast as it had begun, the water calmed and the two eggs popped up like bobbers to the surface. Behind them stretched a trail of pink, blue, yellow and purple tendrils of color that swirled into a rainbow pattern.

Toni clapped her hands. "Oh, I love them. I really, really love them!"

I wished I felt the same way. But I had a creeping, bad feeling, and the things already revolted me.

The phone rang.

"David?" said my mother's voice when I answered. "Is all going well?"

68

"Uh . . . um . . ." I was having a hard time concentrating on the conversation. Even from across the kitchen where the wall phone was mounted, I could see that the two eggs were transforming. One of them had already sprouted a tiny forked tail. And was that a webbed foot I saw?

"David, did you hear me? Is everything all right?"

No, I thought, it's really not. Maybe you should come home right now.

But I kept my mouth shut. I knew how ridiculous that would have sounded. I mean, it was just a novelty toy from a comic book, wasn't it?

"We're great, Mom." I forced myself to sound normal. "Have a good time."

I hung up just as Toni squealed, "Horns! It's got itty-bitty horns!"

After that, things accelerated. The Insta-Pets grew . . . expanded . . . stretched, and then grew some more. Within minutes they were as long as my hand, salmon-colored and plump. Their faces peered at us through the glass, their marble eyes round, dull and flat, their mouths opening and gasping. Just minutes later, they were so big they filled the punch bowl, uncomfortably wedged inside.

"The poor things can't move," said Toni.

And still they kept growing. The little buds of their arms began stretching into tentacles. The little buds on their heads began sprouting into three knobbed horns. Their tails grew longer, fleshier.

"They need more room," declared Toni. "Let's put them in the bathtub."

"No, absolutely not." I gulped as a tentacle flopped over the side of the punch bowl. A webbed hand was just beginning to bloom on the end of it.

As usual, Toni didn't listen. She hurried down the hall to the bathroom and turned on the taps. Water splashed into the tub.

"Didn't you hear me?" I said, going after her. "I said no!"

Ignoring me, she stuck her wrist under the running water, checking the temperature the way you would a baby's bottle. As she adjusted the taps, a yellow rubber duck tipped off the edge of the tub. It hit the water with a squeak. But Toni didn't bother plucking it out. She just bustled off to fetch her pets.

Remembering the instructions' warning about putting things in the water, I reached down to get the duck.

That's when Toni screamed.

I raced into the kitchen. "What is it? What's the matter?"

"We almost killed the poor things, that's the matter!" cried Toni. She pointed.

The Insta-Pets had pulled themselves out of the punch bowl and were writhing and wiggling across the pink countertops. They were as long as my forearm now, translucent and shivering like one of Mom's Jell-O molds.

Toni reached over and grabbed the first one.

It wrapped its immature tentacles around her arms and clung tightly.

"Look, it's hugging me," she cooed.

It didn't remind me of hugging so much as of a boa constrictor squeezing its prey.

Gently, Toni carried it into the bathroom. Prying its tentacles off her arm, she lowered it into the tub. The first Insta-Pet splashed into the water. Moments later, the second one followed. Like some kind of alien squid, they swam around, using their tentacles to inspect their new place. Then they poked their heads above the water, and their mouths opened.

Teeth sprouted like tiny white daggers from their bloodred gums. Just then, two sets of tentacles rose and slithered around the rubber duck. It gave an alarmed squeak before being pulled under. It never re-surfaced.

The doorbell rang.

"Don't put your hands near those things," I warned Toni.

She rolled her eyes. "Honestly, Davey, you're being silly."

"I mean it," I said firmly. "Don't do anything until I get back."

I hurried to the front door, opened it and saw another red box. As I'd done earlier, I stepped onto the porch and looked up and down the street. It was quiet except for Mr. Mayfield washing his Oldsmobile in his driveway and Mr. Humor the ice cream man. Mr. Humor *cha-ching*ed his chrome bicycle bell in greeting as he pedaled past.

Scooping up the box, I turned.

Toni stood in the hallway. "They're gone," she wailed.

"What?" I rushed down the hall, tossing the box into Toni's room as I went.

"I went to get some toys for them to play with—they liked that rubber duck so much," she explained, holding up two plastic dinosaurs. "I was only away for a minute. When I came back—" She pointed.

The bathtub was empty except for six inches of green-tinged water. Two glistening sets of prints trailed across the linoleum floor. Slimy webbed handprints dotted the sill of the now-open window.

"They ran . . . I mean, slithered away," Toni sniffled. "Why would they slither away?"

Before I could come up with an answer, a scream from outside pierced the summer air.

We raced out onto the front porch.

Mrs. Neary hobbled into the street. The left sleeve of her twinset had been ripped clean away, and she was wearing only one high-heeled shoe. "Something took Muffin," she kept repeating like a scratched record. "Something in my backyard. Something took Muffin! Something in my backyard . . ."

She bumped into the curb and just plopped down there, her legs splayed. Her one high heel now dangled drunkenly from her big toe. "Something took Muffin. I heard my little angel howling." Her eyes were wide open, but she stared at nothing. "Something took Muffin."

Beside me, Toni groaned. "Was it . . . do you think?"

I whirled on her. "Of course it was!" I pulled her to the side and through clenched teeth said, "These are not cute pets like hamsters or parakeets. These are some kind of insane mutant Pekingese-chomping monsters!"

Despite herself, Toni giggled. "Pekingese-chomping monsters."

But her laughter died a second later when we saw one of the creatures emerge from between the houses.

"Where's the other one?" she asked.

I shook my head. "I . . . I don't know, but you can bet it's around here someplace."

We crouched behind the porch railing and watched, horrified, as the creature moved through the yards, using the manicured shrubs and white picket fences for cover. Toni's "pet" was now the size of a four-door Buick and covered in translucent pink flesh. We could make out the shapes of its organs, pulsing and fluttering. It dragged itself around upright on two tree-trunk-thick legs that ended in gnarled, clawed feet. As for its webbed hands, they twitched at the ends of two tentacle-like stalks. But it wasn't until the creature lifted its head that I felt the bile rise in my throat. On its face was fixed a smile, permanent and corrupt—a yellow-fanged gash curving under eyes as dead as eight balls.

I sucked in my breath. "It can't be."

But it was—

Just like in those pictures on the Insta-Pet kit's envelopes, a red bow decorated the monster's three knobbed horns!

*Cha-ching! Cha-ching! Cha-ching!* The sound of Mr. Humor's bicycle bell rang through the air.

The monster dropped behind a bush, crouched, became statue still. It cocked its hideous head to the right, listening, then flicked its forked tail. A black tongue, slimy and dripping, slicked its grinning lips. Then it focused its gaze on the ice cream man, who unknowingly pedaled straight toward its hiding place.

"Oh my God," I whimpered. Then I was running down the sidewalk, my bare feet pounding on the pavement.

"Mr. Humor!" I yelled. "Stop! Stop!"

But it was too late.

A fleshy tentacle whipped from behind the bush and lifted Mr. Humor off his bicycle seat. A second tentacle wrapped around his waist, and I caught a flash of the creature's hideous underside. It was a gray color like rotten meat, and it was dotted with hundreds of fluttering, hungry suckers.

Mr. Humor's eyes bulged. "Get him off me!" he shrieked. "Please, get him off me!"

I lunged and grabbed Mr. Humor by his ankles. I pulled as hard as I could, falling onto the street, using my legs for leverage—straining, panting.

Mr. Humor struggled, grabbing the bike's handle. He held it tightly, his knuckles turning white as the monster tightened its grip.

I tugged with all my might, feeling as if my arms might tear off.

The monster's forked tail whipped around and slithered over my skin. I shuddered as the cold and pulsating thing slipped around Mr. Humor's neck.

"Help me!" sobbed the ice cream man as the creature ripped him from my grasp.

It raised Mr. Humor to its weirdly smiling mouth.

Mr. Humor kicked frantically, knocking off one of his canvas shoes. It arced through the air, landing in the middle of the street, clean and white. Then the ice cream man screamed, and the shoe was suddenly splattered with blood. There came a wet, crunching sound, and his fingers slowly released their grip on the bike handle. The bike fell and the cooler unit smashed open, sending Popsicles and ice cream sandwiches skittering across the pavement.

The bell let out one final *cha-ching.*

The creature burped.

Mr. Humor was gone.

And then there was no sound at all, except for the rasping of my breath and the soft, slithery sound of the monster as it squirmed across the melting treats and through Mrs. Ivey's yard.

I was sure I was dessert. But the creature didn't turn

back. It never even looked at me. It just slid on past as I lay curled into a numb, terrified ball in the middle of the street.

Then I heard another sound—a soft, sobbing sound.

Toni stood on the sidewalk, her round face deadly pale except for her huge dark eyes. They were shiny with tears.

"This is all my fault!" she cried pitifully.

I dragged myself up off the pavement and over to her. "We can't think about that now," I said. I was in shock, but the look in Toni's eyes, her little face so full of pain, galvanized me. "We have to get help."

We stumbled back to the house and into the kitchen. I snatched up the phone.

Silence.

"It's dead!" I cried.

Toni looked bewildered. "That makes no sense. Do Insta-Pets know about phone wires?"

The sunroom door began to rattle on its hinges. One of the monsters pressed its grotesque face to the glass. Which one was it? And—dear God—where was the other one?

I grabbed Toni's arm. "Come on, we've got to get out of here and get help!"

We raced across an expanse of gold carpeting toward the front door.

But at that very moment the picture window in the living room was darkened by the mass of the second monster. It was peering in, drooling, with something furry and white between its teeth.

"That's Mr. Kopecky's cat," said Toni. "Aw, poor Bubbles!"

And then from the sunroom came an explosion of breaking glass and splintering rattan furniture. A moment later the first monster lurched into the kitchen.

The second monster pressed hard against the living room window. Tiny cracks began to radiate from the corners of the glass.

In the split second before we bolted down the hall, I noticed something that made my blood turn cold. The second monster was wearing cowboy boots just like in that picture on the envelope. No, these weren't baby Insta-Pets anymore. Not cute cartoons in a comic book. These were fully formed man-and-pet-eating monsters.

We raced into Toni's bedroom. Heaving and panting, we shoved her Pink Princess vanity table across the door, then headed for the window.

It wouldn't budge.

"Come on," I groaned, beating on the sill, the frame, the glass.

We could hear the scrape and slither of the monsters in the hall.

"Davey? What do we do?" cried Toni.

There was no time for plans. The monsters had already reached the door and were pushing and grunting against it. We could hear their teeth gnashing like saw blades and smell the sickening mixture of grape Popsicle and blood. One of the tentacles flattened and swept under the door. It slid between the vanity's legs, groping. . . . It grabbed Toni's Wetty Betty doll, seemed to examine it by touch, then released it. Its webbed hand bumped into my bare toe, and I jumped back. The movement excited the monster. It closed around Toni's teddy bear. It squeezed. Stuffing exploded.

"Pookie!" yelped Toni.

A forked tail joined the tentacle in searching, grabbing, squeezing. Books and board games scattered, the *Sky King* bedside lamp bounced once and shattered, and in a sickening crunch the little man on top of Toni's peewee bowling trophy was pounded into shards.

The tentacle reached for her Chrissie Dream Cottage.

"Not Chrissie!" Toni screamed. Snatching up a tennis racket, she forehanded the tentacle. *Thwack!*

The tentacle grabbed the racket and squeezed. Wood and strings flew. And now the forked tail was back. It swept across the bed, knocking a package to the floor, seizing a pillow. Feathers filled the air.

Even in the chaos, I noticed the red box.

"Toni!" I shouted. "What else did you order out of your magazine?"

"Huh?" She was ducking and jumping, trying desperately to stay out of the monster's reach.

The vanity table began to move across the bedroom floor. Wood and plaster cracked. We had only seconds.

"Tell me now!" I shouted, beating at the tentacle with a Happy Trails hairbrush.

Toni clambered onto her matching Pink Princess dresser to escape the flailing tail. It followed her, pulling out drawers. Socks and underpants flew.

"What's in the box?" I screamed again.

From her perch, she said, "Um . . . uh . . . let me think."

The door was ripped from its hinges.

"Um . . . a pair of X-ray glasses, a Hypno-Coin, onion gum, a crystal ball, a Captain Gizmo atomic ray gun, and—"

Lunging across the room, I snatched the package out from under a shredded Snuffy Town bedspread just as the door burst open. The monsters stood there, staring, smiling. . . .

I clawed at the package's wrapping. Please, God, I begged, please don't let it be the onion gum!

The monsters slithered across the floor, suction cups fluttering eagerly. We were trapped.

Toni jumped off the dresser. Placing herself between the monsters and me, she began hurling anything and everything at them—her poodle skirt, her *Howdy Doody* ventriloquist dummy, even her Elvis Presley records. "Go away! Get back!"

I pulled back the box flaps.

It wasn't the onion gum!

"Get out of the way!" I shouted at Toni.

She turned, saw what I was holding and instantly

understood. She rolled to the left side as I raised the Captain Gizmo Atomic Ray Gun, aimed at the first monster and pulled the trigger. The ray gun crackled, flared red and let out a loud *dat-dat-dat-dat!*

The first monster exploded in a cloud of black goop, splattering the Pink Princess wallpaper.

I pointed the gun at the second monster.

*Dat-dat-dat-dat!*

It exploded, too—a spewing fountain of black gore, teeth and suckers.

"We did it!" shouted Toni, hurling herself into my arms. "We did it!"

I dropped the ray gun and, whooping, whirled her around and around.

That's when I felt something wet and rubbery twist around my ankle.

A tentacle rose from behind me and coiled around my legs. The slimy flesh tightened, squeezed, tugged. I could feel its rows of suckers tearing my skin. I turned and saw the thing. It was like the others—fork-tailed and tentacled—but its body was different . . . yellow . . . rounder . . . like . . . *a huge rubber duck!* I had time for one thought—DO NOT ADD ANY INGREDIENTS BUT OFFICIAL INSTA-PETS PRODUCTS TO YOUR PETS' WATER—before it grabbed me. I screamed, lightning bolts of pain radiating out to my fingertips and down to my toes. It had me, and I was being eaten alive. *Eaten alive!*

Toni shrieked, hitting at the new monster with her bare fists.

"The ray gun!" I screamed.

She dropped to her knees, scrabbling through the debris of clothes and games and exploded stuffed animals.

The second tentacle whipped around my head, covering my mouth.

"Help me!" I tried to scream, but it came out a muffled moan.

The suckers were doing a vicious dance on my neck and face now, feasting on my skin, dissolving my flesh. The room began to grow dark. My breath came in weak puffs. I felt myself being lifted, tilted. I could smell the creature's putrid breath, could hear—even through the hammering of my own heart—the gnashing and grinding of its teeth.

*Dat-dat-dat-dat!*

I dropped to the floor, splashing hard into a sticky pile of goo.

But I knew it was too late.

Toni dropped to her knees beside me. Although she was nothing more than a dark blur, I could hear her voice and feel the touch of her hand in mine. I could feel her tears dripping onto my ravaged face, too.

What was left of my mouth opened and closed like a dying goldfish. Strange, but I had always thought it would be a Russian A-bomb or a UFO that would get me in the end. Who would ever have imagined a comic-book novelty?

"David, oh, David," Toni sobbed.

I squeezed her hand weakly to reassure her. My sister was safe, and that was all that really mattered. I let my fingers relax.

"You must have cared deeply for your sister." It was the girl in the long skirt. She was seated on an urn-shaped gravestone, and in the moonlight the tear slipping down her cheek glimmered like a tiny crystal.

David, his expression stricken, nodded.

"I had a sister, too," the girl said. "Her name was Blanche. But I did not care for her." She shook her head. "No, I did not care for her, not one little bit. . . ."

# EVELYN

## 1877–1893

**A** FIERCE CHICAGO WIND ROARED off the lake that day, rattling the white buildings of the World's Fair with rude, jostling whooshes. For one moment it settled—ah, calm at last, I thought—before puckishly rising again, more tempestuous than before.

I watched as fairgoers scampered along the winding pathways seeking refuge. According to the *Chicago Daily Tribune*, more than fourteen million visitors had already flocked here to experience the eye-catching wonders of the World's Columbian Exposition—more commonly known as the Chicago World's Fair. All across the country, Americans were mortgaging their farms and houses, borrowing money on their life insurance or trimming their Christmas budgets to save for the trip, convinced there would be nothing like it for at least another hundred years. And few, it seemed, regretted their sacrifices. Just the other day I had read about an Iowa farmer who—after gazing openmouthed at Edison's Tower of Light with its zigzagging, flashing bulbs—said to his wife, "Well, Susan, it paid, even if it did take all the burial money."

Today's weather, however, was wreaking havoc with the fairgoers' fun. Some ducked into the immense Illinois Building to catch their breaths. Others sought protection in Machinery Hall or girded themselves against the blustery gusts with a stein of beer at the German Village. But the wind always found them. Shoving. Pushing. Snatching off hats and blowing up skirts.

Already this evening's fireworks had been rescheduled, and the movable sidewalk that jutted into Lake Michigan was shut down because of the whitecaps breaking over it. I had even heard rumors that Buffalo Bill's Wild West Show would be canceled.

Such a shame! I would have sincerely loved seeing my sister, Blanche, get trampled by a herd of stampeding bison.

"I cannot believe this weather, and on the day *I* decide to attend the fair," Blanche fretted, fumbling with her parasol. It might have been windy, but the sun beating down on us was a hot July one.

Just as soon as she opened her parasol, though, the wind snatched it from her lace-gloved hands. It flew out over the North Pond like a fleeing raven.

I giggled.

"I fail to see the humor," said Blanche in her usual

nose-in-the-air tone. "I'll be baked crispy as a farm-hand if I don't escape this dreadful sun."

I imagined a curl of smoke rising from a charred, withered thing. Blanche baked to a crisp. Delightful!

Blanche noted my pleasure.

"Sister dear," she said oh so sweetly, "you're positively *dewy*." She offered me one of her lace-edged hand-kerchiefs. It smelled of rose water. "Really, Evelyn, you sweat so profusely one might think you were a common laborer." And with that bit of nastiness, she sailed off.

I stood there, hating her. I think I had always hated my twin sister—since that day, sixteen years ago last month, when we were born.

Blanche came first, of course, shoving me aside so she could make her dramatic entrance into the world. The firstborn. The special one.

"She had such wide blue eyes," Mother once recalled when I asked about that day, "and such translucent alabaster skin. The midwife claimed she'd never seen such a beautiful infant."

"What about me?" I begged. "What do you remember about me?"

"You were different from Blanche," Mother said. "So small and dark. We were"—she fumbled for the word—"startled."

Something cold and bitter began nibbling at my insides.

Did anyone coo over me when I appeared minutes later? I longed to ask. Did they marvel at my skin, too?

Admire my eyes? I guessed not. As always, Blanche had seized all the attention for herself.

As we grew, our differences became more pronounced. Blanche was all golden light. I was dingy and plump. Blanche glowed with wit and laughter. I preferred to keep to myself. Blanche was all cultured breeding. I detested putting on airs.

"Like day and night," Father often said.

"More like Beauty and the Beast," Blanche would taunt behind his back.

That was Blanche—sweet kisses and pretty smiles in public, hisses and torment when we were alone together.

Now Blanche turned, the wind snapping at her skirts. "Come *on,* Evelyn." She pressed her *Handbook of the World's Columbian Exposition* to her chest to keep its hundreds of pages from ruffling. "Honestly, you dodder like an old man. We won't have time to see a thing if you don't hurry up."

What she meant was that we wouldn't have time to see all the things *she* wanted to see. If I'd had my druthers, we'd have been walking along the Midway Plaisance, a mile-long stretch of the exotic and miraculous—Persian belly dancers, Hindu jugglers and, of course, Mr. Ferris's big steel wheel. I heard there was even a wax museum where one could see Marie Antoinette about to be guillotined.

I studied Blanche's delicate neck. A charming picture sprang to mind.

Earlier that morning at breakfast, Blanche had haughtily announced, "I have decided on our itinerary." She had dropped the thick handbook onto the linen-covered table, causing Mother's bone china to rattle. "We will take in the lace and embroidery demonstration at the Manufactures and Liberal Arts Building, followed by a lecture about silkworms at the Horticulture Building, and then refreshments in the ladies' tearoom at the Woman's Building. Afterward we will tour the Palace of Fine Arts, where some of the fair's most culturally significant exhibits can be found."

"That sounds very sensible, Blanche," Father had said, bestowing an indulgent smile on her. "An enlightening day indeed."

"What about the chocolate Venus de Milo?" I had asked. "What about the eleven-ton cheese?"

Blanche had pretended to be shocked. "Really, Evelyn, those sorts of exhibits are for the riffraff. We are going to the fair to absorb its grace and refinement." She gave a superior-sounding laugh. "Sometimes you can be so common."

"But . . . but . . . ," I had stammered.

"Mind your sister, dear," Mother had said. "She's been studying the guide. I'm sure she is only interested in elevating your aesthetic sensibilities." Mother had been listening to Blanche's plan with a rapt expression. Why didn't she ever look at me that way?

"Indeed, Evelyn," said Blanche, a snakelike smile

slithering onto her face, "when it comes to erudition, I *do* know best."

Gritting my teeth, I lifted my butter knife and hacked my hard-boiled egg into pieces.

Hours later, the morning's breakfast conversation still rankled. Grudgingly, I quickened my pace. Blanche and I walked directly into the wind, weaving in and out of the crowd and crossing an ornate footbridge. As we passed a fountain of Pegasus, colored water spewing from its mouth, the wind gusted again. Water sprinkled over us, tickling our cheeks and freckling our dresses. I squealed with delight, but Blanche looked as if she had just swallowed a sour grape. "This wind is absolutely maddening. Just look at what it's done!"

She was still grumbling and brushing at the red silk skirt she had so fastidiously picked out in the morning, when we arrived at the Palace of Fine Arts. The guarding stone lions observed us as we climbed the steep marble stairs and entered the columned exhibit hall.

Even inside, there was little escape from the wind. Doors and windows shook. Walls groaned. At any moment, I thought, the place could crumble as easily as one of Mother's sugar cookies. I looked up to the ceiling, to the sweeping gilded cupola that had been imported all the way from an Italian monastery. I imagined it crashing into a golden heap on the marble floor, leaving one of Blanche's lace-gloved hands jutting from the rubble.

Blanche's hand.

I suppressed a giggle.

Blanche moved through the massive exhibition space, taking in Winslow Homer's swirling seascapes and Mary Cassatt's tender portraits as if she was searching for something. No doubt it was some wearisome objet d'art she had read about in her precious handbook. I could just hear her bragging to our parents, "And did I tell you I saw Daniel Chester French's *The Angel of Death and the Sculptor*? I admired it ever so much. Sadly, Evelyn appeared unmoved." She'd roll her eyes. "I believe she even yawned."

I narrowed my eyes at her.

And Blanche rearranged her expression. That searching look disappeared, replaced by a perfect imitation of the intent, absorbed expression worn by the other art lovers. Feigning sophistication, she glided about, peering at canvases and into glass cases. But she was fully aware of the admiring looks several of the young men in the hall were giving her. I was disgusted to see her widen her eyes and tilt her head. She posed prettily, utterly pleased with herself.

No one admired me, of course. Who would, with Blanche around? Turning away from her, I drifted toward the grand staircase. "Don't get separated," Father had warned before we left. "Be sure to stay together."

But some demon was tugging at me, urging me to be perverse. Deliberately, willfully, without even a backward glance, I climbed to the second-floor landing. A suit of armor guarding the long corridor stared down at me accusingly as if it sensed my oozing, spiteful mood. I stuck my tongue out at it, then headed down the corridor—farther and farther away from Blanche—through a seemingly endless array of bucolic landscapes and elegant portraits. After several minutes' walk, I found myself at a mahogany-inlaid door, which I pushed open to discover a narrow flight of twisting stairs made of wrought iron. A red velvet rope was draped between the railings; a sign hanging from its center read DO NOT ENTER. Undisturbed by the warning, I unhooked the rope. The steps, I noticed, were layered with dust, as if they had remained unused since the fair had opened three months earlier. Curious, I lifted my skirt and climbed to the third-floor gallery, then on to the fourth.

Up there, so close to the roof of the building, the wind howled. It forced its way under the eaves and whistled through the chinks in the plaster, causing the heavy Moroccan curtains—draped from the ceiling to cover the windows and darken the gallery—to undulate like seaweed. The whole room felt as if it was moving, as if I was standing on one of those double-decker steamers that plied the Chicago River. I took a moment to get my bearings, poised there alone while just below, hundreds of people jostled in the main hall. Was I really the only person who had felt compelled to climb those stairs?

I looked around. The gallery was a profusion of carved furniture and gilt-edged knickknacks set about in a hodgepodge. As I made my way through the maze of artifacts, I glanced at the handwritten cards identifying each piece: Mozart's spinet, the King of Bavaria's water goblets, Catherine the Great's hairpins.

Hanging against the shadowy back wall was a gold frame. I could not make out what was inside the frame because its surface was concealed behind a red velvet drapery. But suddenly I was overwhelmed with a need to know what lay beneath. I *had* to see it. It was as mysterious as a crime waiting to be solved, as tantalizing as a gift begging to be opened.

THE CONTARINI LOOKING GLASS, read its card.

I reached out, intending to lift just a corner of the drapery.

"That would be ill advised, mademoiselle."

I pulled back my hand, startled to see a man who seemed to have appeared out of nowhere. He hurried forward, waving his chubby arms emphatically before him.

"You should not gaze into the Contarini Looking Glass!"

The man reminded me of a walrus, with his bristly mustache and barrel chest. He even wobbled rather than walked. But most astonishing was his clothing. He was wearing a tuxedo—a *purple* tuxedo—with silver lapels and waistcoat. On his egg-shaped head was balanced a matching purple turban, its folds of cloth held together in the front by a fist-sized gold pin shaped like a human eye.

My own eyes widened. "Who are you?" I asked.

"Moreau the Mystical—Soothsayer, Hypnotist and Grand Illusionist—formerly of Algeria, currently of the Midway Plaisance."

I smiled. That explained his dramatic entrance—he was a magician! Delighted, I wondered if he could make Blanche disappear into thin air—or even better, saw her in half.

"I am here, mademoiselle, because you are in grave danger." He squeezed himself between the mirror and me. "For your own protection, I must insist that you step back."

"Step back?" I asked. "Whatever for?"

"Because this mirror"—he lowered his voice—"is evil."

I could not help laughing. "Evil? Why, we're on the brink of the twentieth century, sir. No one believes in curses and superstitions anymore."

"Oh, no?" he said, waggling his bushy eyebrows. "Why else would such a priceless objet d'art be hidden away in this forgotten fourth-floor gallery, eh? And why is its face completely covered? Because, mademoiselle, the Contarini Looking Glass is too dangerous to exhibit to the masses. Because someone, Heaven forbid, might look into it and see . . . death."

Around us the wind moaned. The curtains rose and fell. The room seemed to breathe.

"The mirror dates back to 1631," said the magician, "when a glassmaker of little ability but limitless ambition named Alessandro Contarini began creating magnificent mirrors. Masterpieces of genius they were, mademoiselle, with the clarity of flawless diamonds and glass as smooth as the Venetian lagoon in springtime. Overnight, Contarini became the most celebrated and sought-after mirror maker in all of Europe. Everyone—from cantina owners to the King of France—longed to possess one of his creations. But those who knew him best were suspicious. 'How can this be?' his fellow craftsmen wondered. 'How can hapless Alessandro have suddenly acquired such knowledge and skill?' It was, they all agreed, most curious. Then one All Hallows' Eve, Contarini's neighbors heard him screaming in agony. When they finally managed to break down his workshop door, they found . . . nothing! No furniture. No tools. No Contarini. The room was empty save for a single mirror angled against the rough plaster wall." Moreau pointed. "*That* mirror."

I stared at the draped object as if hypnotized.

Finally, I asked, "What happened to Contarini? Did anyone ever find him?"

Moreau shook his head. "There were clues only: a curious five-pointed star crudely drawn on his bedroom floor; beneath a loosened floorboard, an unusual document that smelled of sulfur and was signed by the glassmaker himself."

"You're not suggesting that he made a bargain . . . ," I began, hardly able to contain my excitement.

"That Contarini made a bargain with the devil?" said Moreau with a shrug. "Who is to say?"

The wind whistled again, and the curtains danced to its tune.

"Over the years, the mirror has been associated with several other odd and unfortunate incidents. There was the avaricious Italian princess who demanded more and more priceless jewelry; the obese colonial governor who lived only for his next meal; the lazy French duke who refused to leave the comfort of his bed. All of them looked into that mirror and"—Moreau snapped his fingers—"vanished like Contarini."

"Surely it was all just coincidence."

Moreau shook his head. "Do you not see it, mademoiselle? The pattern? The mirror reflects whatever darkness may be in the viewer's heart and *feeds* upon it—Contarini's lust for fame, the princess's greed, the governor's gluttony, the duke's laziness. Sin and darkness. This is what it seeks, what sustains and nourishes it."

"How do you know? How can you be so sure?"

His mouth quirked. "I am a master of illusion. I know about mirrors."

We fell silent, the only sound the unceasing wind.

"And I warn you, this mirror is hungry," he added.

At that moment, a new image sprang—unbidden—into my head. It was of Blanche, smiling vainly at her lovely reflection, while a death-white arm reached from the mirror. Its bony fingers stretched, groped, curled around her white neck.

I shivered, but not with pleasure. This was not some idle daydream, like stampeding bison and falling cupolas. This felt real—thick and poisonous and true.

"Evelyn!"

I whirled. It was Blanche's annoyed call, coming from the staircase—that twisting iron staircase that no one had climbed but me.

And now her.

It was as if my very thoughts had drawn her here, through the maze of corridors and exhibits, to this very place.

My thoughts, I suddenly wondered, or the mirror's?

I turned back to Moreau, the question already on my lips, but he was gone. Vanished as mysteriously as he had appeared. My body chilled and then began to burn as I realized the truth. He had left me alone with the mirror and its obvious intentions—left *me* to make the choice that would determine my sister's fate.

But I was given no time to think. At that exact moment, Blanche appeared in the doorway. Oh, if only she had uttered one kind word, offered one soft look!

She did not.

"There you are," she huffed; the milky-white skin of her neck was blotched red with anger. "Honestly, Evelyn, why didn't you answer when I called? I have been searching all over for you. Really, you are the most petulant, irritating, troublesome person."

A coldness descended over me, hard and icy. I watched her, as if from a distance, as she stepped into the cluttered gallery, her bright eyes taking in the jumble of artifacts. "What is that beneath the velvet curtain?" she asked at last. She pointed to the far wall.

I felt a faint stir of excitement in my breast.

"I haven't the foggiest."

She moved across the room, confident as always, and peered at the card. " 'The Contarini Looking Glass,' " she read aloud. "Hmmm . . . I wonder why it's covered?"

It took all my willpower not to smile. "It must be a very ordinary object if it is covered like that," I said, knowing full well that Blanche would find it impossible to pass up this opportunity to belittle me.

"Poor Evelyn, you really don't know anything, do you?" she said, and sighed dramatically. "One usually covers up the most *exceptional* and delicate artwork for safekeeping. Let's take a look, shall we?"

"Yes, let's!" I could not keep the giggle out of my voice.

Smugly, Blanche reached for the drapery.

The wind blew again, rustling the velvet drape, giving the illusion that some creature slithered beneath. I laughed, a weird, high-pitched laugh that welled up, unbidden, from the frozen depths of my soul. Yes, yes, she was going to do it. It would not be long now. In just a matter of moments she would be—

Without warning, my laughter turned to wails—howling, hysterical wailing that drowned out even the wind. God help me, I could not do it! Despite all the years of humiliation and torment, I could not murder my sister.

"No!" I gripped Blanche's shoulders and yanked her away from the mirror with such force that we both lost our balance. Blanche reached out and grabbed at the mirror for support but got a handful of the red drapery instead. With a horrible tearing sound, it gave way, pooling onto the carpet like blood.

"Don't look into the mirror!" I cried.

But it was too late. In its flawless surface Blanche stared at her lovely face, transfixed by her own reflection. "Didn't I tell you so, Evelyn? This mirror is exceptional." She turned to admire her profile from the left, and then the right. She smiled at herself, sure and proud of her beauty. *The sin of vanity.*

And the mirror began to draw her in. Little by little, she withdrew into the glass as if sinking into a pool of darkening water.

Fixing my eyes on her face, refusing even to look in the mirror's direction, I grabbed her about the waist. I pulled with all my strength, but gained no ground. She sank deeper and deeper. I was losing her!

Her lips were still pressed into a smile, although her eyes were no longer filled with self-admiration. Now they were welling up with fear and confusion. But she did not struggle. It was as if she was frozen, becoming as solid as the surface of the glass. And yet she was still beautiful. So beautiful. All golden perfection. The special one.

*It was so unfair.*

And suddenly, behind Blanche's diminishing reflection, I saw my own—raw envy etched into my expression.

*The sin of envy.*

Unable to tear my eyes away, I could only stare deep into the mirror.

Now the gallery was reflected to me, everything distorted and listing crazily. The curtains billowed and undulated. The wind moaned. And I felt the grip of the mirror. Its embrace was strangely warm. Gentle. So gentle. My mind objected, but my body surrendered. I felt myself descending, disappearing.

But before I was entirely gone, I willed myself to do one last thing—something I had never done before. With my last ounce of strength, I reached out and found Blanche's hand in the growing darkness. I grasped it. A heartbeat passed; then her lace-covered fingers entwined with mine.

We had come into the world separately.

But we would leave together.

The mist was deeper now, lying over the cemetery like a shroud, and from the deep shadows emerged another girl. Mike blinked. Why hadn't he noticed her before? She, too, had on a long skirt, but where Evelyn's was gray and simply made, this girl's was red, elaborately ruffled and topped by a lace blouse and matching gloves.

"Blanche?" ventured Mike.

The ghost smiled prettily, then moved confidently through the swirling mist to sit beside her sister on the urn-shaped stone. "You told the story extremely well, Evelyn. I couldn't have done better myself." Reaching up, she wiped away Evelyn's crystalline tears. "Honestly, I don't know why you're crying."

"Because it is sad," said Evelyn. "It is a sad story."

"Sad?" guffawed Johnnie. "You dames deserved what you got."

Scott sighed. "Let's not start *that* again."

"Death stories are always sad," interjected Gina. "No matter if it's murder, or monsters, or arson, they're all sad."

"It's not the events that make them sad," said Scott, "it's what they represent."

Johnnie raised his eyebrows. "Come again, wise guy?"

"Our lives ended way too early," explained Scott. "Think of all the things we missed out on. All the things we'll never experience."

"Like learning to drive a car," said David, his voice full of disappointment.

"Or going to college," Scott added wistfully.

"I refuse to think about it," said Evelyn. She jumped

to her feet. "The only way to bear it is to *not* think about it."

"Dead and gone," whispered Johnnie.

The cemetery grew so quiet, Mike could hear himself breathing. There was no other sound now. Not the moaning of the wind, or the creaking of a tree branch. He felt the ghosts' sadness and longing deep within his own bones and wished he could help them. But there was nothing he could do, nothing except . . .

"Does anyone else have a story to tell?" he asked.

A girl stepped into the circle of moonlight. "I do."

# LILY

## 1982–1999

IT WASN'T A CRUSH. It wasn't puppy love. I knew what love was—*real* love. After all, I'd been reading about it for years—*Much Ado About Nothing, Romeo and Juliet, Love's Labour's Lost.* In fact, I'd read all thirty-seven of Shakespeare's plays and all one hundred and fifty-four of his sonnets. You could say I'd gorged myself on Shakespeare (which is way better than gorging yourself on a bag of Milky Way miniatures), and if there was one thing I knew after all that reading, it was this: I *loved* Collin. With all my heart. And I knew I would love him until the end of time.

> *Did my heart love till now?*
> *Forswear it, sight!*
> *For I ne'er saw true beauty*
> *till this night!*

We didn't meet until our senior year—not surprising, considering there were about three thousand kids at Schaumburg High School. Our paths never crossed, fate never intervened, until the semester we both signed up for drama class—me because of my obsession with the Bard of Avon, Collin because he needed an honors elective.

"Lily," said Mrs. Childress on our second day of class, "would you read the role of Juliet, please?"

I cleared my throat, took a moment to think—*really* think—about the music of William Shakespeare's passionate words.

*O Romeo, Romeo! Wherefore art thou Romeo?*

I paused then, and looked up from the page. And there he was! *My* Romeo, *my* Collin. He sat by the window wearing a pair of tan cargo pants and a yellow-and-green-striped rugby shirt, his black hair glinting in the afternoon sunlight, his lips as red and inviting as the apple I'd had for lunch.

As usual, I was on a diet.

Oh, and his eyes. Did I tell you about his eyes? They were a brilliant blue, but not the blue of my favorite Abercrombie dress, the one that looked a little like the outfit Cleopatra was wearing the day she kissed Antony goodbye for the last time. No, Collin's eyes were a brimming blue, as if on the verge of tears, and the sunlight streaming through the window danced on that blue like shimmer on a lake.

There are moments that stop the heart, you know?

Moments that seize your breath and halt the flow of your blood in your veins, and the clock stops—time stops—and you wait for something to bring you back again. And what brought me back was my name on his lips:

"Lily? What are you staring at? Do I have food in my teeth or something?"

*O, speak again, bright angel!*

And I knew. Just like Romeo knew the first time he beheld Juliet, or like Petruchio when he spied shrewish Katharina hurling a vase. Love had come crashing across the cosmos. Unknown. Unhoped for. Unexpected. Yet in a twinkling I understood that *this* was forever.

I stumbled through the rest of the passage, through the rest of the period. Then the bell rang and he crossed the room toward me. *For me.* His aftershave, spicy and exotic, invaded my senses, making my heart pulse wildly and my head whirl.

"Want to hang out tonight?" he asked.

I wanted to leap with joy, or run around in circles, or sing a song, or write a poem.

"Yes," I whispered, because I couldn't speak any louder.

*No sooner met, but they looked; no sooner looked*
*but they loved; no sooner loved but they sighed.*

After that day, Collin and I were always together—in the school cafeteria, in the hallway between classes, at the movies, the mall, each other's houses. We carried each other's pictures in our wallets; spent Sunday after-noons bicycling together through Busse Woods; read to each other from our favorite books—mine *The Complete Works of William Shakespeare,* Collin's *The Complete Calvin and Hobbes.* We discovered that it drove Collin nuts when I clicked my pen against my teeth while studying. We agreed that it was okay for me to listen to Sarah McLachlan and for him to listen to Jay-Z just as long as the other person wasn't around. And we figured out that Collin should always stop for our soy sugar-free cinnamon dolce lattes *before* picking me up for school because I wasn't a morning person, and that I should bake snicker doodles for him at least once a month because they were his absolute favorite—another of true love's sacrifices because I was, like I said, dieting.

And then?

Life shattered.

We were coming home from the library that Saturday—Collin and me and his younger brother, Drew, when we saw a clutch of leftover birthday balloons waving from a mailbox. A handmade sign propped against a harvest-gold recliner read GARAGE SALE. Beyond it, a ton of junk stretched from the depths of a double garage, out onto the driveway and across the expanse of lawn.

*All that glisters is not gold.*

Drew leaned over the front seat, a lock of his dark hair falling over the sprinkling of acne that had just recently cropped up on his forehead. "Hey, c'mon, you guys, let's stop," he begged.

Drew had a real thing for garage sales, especially the half-built car model kits you could sometimes find at them. Afterward, he would spend hours putting all those tiny plastic pieces together, the nostril-searing stink of model glue oozing out from under his bedroom door.

"Do you think my brother's a nerd?" Collin had once asked me.

"Yes," I had replied, "but a sweet nerd."

Now Collin pulled over to the curb. He had barely stopped before Drew had the door open and was loping away in hot pursuit of treasure. We followed along behind, hand in hand, happy just to be together.

A dozen or so people milled around. Some poked through the racks of out-of-style dresses and jackets; others riffled through laundry baskets of used kitchen utensils or pawed over piles of stained baby clothes. I looked around for the stack of paperback books. Every garage sale has them, and sometimes I could actually find a dog-eared copy of *Macbeth*, or the CliffsNotes version of *All's Well That Ends Well*. That's when I caught a glimpse of myself in a dresser mirror.

"Tell me the truth," I said to Collin, "do I look fat to you?"

"You're kidding, right?" he said, kissing my forehead.

"No, seriously."

Collin's eyes sparkled. "If you're fat, you're fat in all the right places."

I poked him in the stomach just as Drew hollered,

"Hey, guys, check *this* out." Stumbling around the tired furniture and jumbled tables of mismatched silverware and cast-off jewelry, he held out something dark and gnarled.

The thing was a knot of furrowed leather that sprouted five wrinkled fingers, each tipped with a cracked yellow nail. The fingers curved into a sort of agonized claw—a hideous mummy's claw fringed with long black fur.

"What is it?" said Collin.

"*That* is a genuine, bona fide monkey's paw," came a voice from behind us.

We turned.

The garage sale's organizer stood there, a plump middle-aged woman wearing a red velour sweat suit and gold sandals. She had just put on fresh lipstick, and when she grinned at us, her mouth looked like it was bleeding.

"*Double, double toil and trouble,*" I muttered under my breath.

"A monkey's paw," she repeated. "You don't find many of those around."

"Thank goodness," I said with a shudder.

"Isn't there some law about hacking off a monkey's hand?" asked Collin.

I imagined a jungle full of one-handed monkeys falling from the trees. "If there isn't, there should be," I said.

We waited for Drew to agree, but he just stood there. By the way he was clutching the paw, I could tell he wanted it.

"How much?" he asked.

"Twenty dollars," the woman replied after a moment's thought. "I'll be honest with you. I started at seventy-five, but nobody's shown any interest in it."

"No wonder—it's hideous," I said under my breath. "Drew, you're not really going to spend money on that thing, are you?"

But Drew was already digging in his pocket.

"What about your car fund?" Collin reminded him. "I thought you were saving every cent between now and your sixteenth birthday for a"—he imitated Drew's slightly lisping voice—"dope set of wheels?"

Drew was as obsessed with classic cars as he was with modeling kits. Every inch of his bedroom walls was covered with posters of Impalas, Mustangs, Camaros, Trans Ams. I'd once asked him why he never taped up any pictures of new ones. "Cars from the seventies are my passion," he'd replied.

Now I said, "Think about that Mustang, Drew."

"Or that GTO," added Collin.

Drew hesitated, then whipped out his wallet decisively. "How often does a guy get the chance at a real monkey paw, huh?" He looked at the woman. "Do you know anything about it?"

"Just what I heard from Mr. Patel," she replied. "He's

the one who gave it to me. Of course, I don't believe a word he said." She lowered her voice to a whisper, twirling her finger around her ear. "He just wasn't himself after the house fire, if you know what I mean."

"House fire?" repeated Drew. He laid a handful of crumpled dollars on the table, then began counting out his loose change.

She pointed her chin at the empty lot across the street. "Mr. Patel's house stood right there until the fire. Everything he owned went up in flames—everything except that monkey paw. When he saw it, he said, 'Take it, Mrs. Alvarez. Bury it, burn it, throw it in the lake—*anything*. I just never want to lay eyes on it again.' "

"Why not?" I wondered.

"That's what I asked him, and he said the paw was magic."

Drew stroked the paw's fur. "Magic, huh?"

"Old magic, according to Mr. Patel," said Mrs. Alvarez, snorting with disbelief. "Seems that hundreds of years ago an East Indian fakir—you know, a holy man—put a spell on the paw. 'The fakir wanted people to understand that fate ruled their lives,' Mr. Patel tells me all serious-like, 'and that those who tried to interfere with their fate would meet great sorrow.' So the fakir put a spell on the paw—whoever owned it could have three wishes granted from it." Mrs. Alvarez snorted again. "Isn't that the most ridiculous thing you've ever heard? Sounds like something from some kids' book, doesn't it?"

She didn't wait for us to answer, just plowed on.

"I couldn't help myself, now, could I? I had to ask. 'Did you make your wishes?' I ask Mr. Patel. 'Were they granted?' And you know, Mr. Patel's face turned white as a corpse. He looked toward the ruin of his house, just stared at it for a while. Then he slowly nodded. 'They were,' he says to me, moaning. 'God help me, they were.' Then he threw the paw down. 'Get rid of it, Mrs. Alvarez. Do this last favor for me and destroy it.'"

"But you didn't," I said. "Destroy it, I mean."

"Of course not! Why throw away something that might make a little money?" Mrs. Alvarez turned her attention to the pile of coins and bills Drew had put in front of her. After counting it—her bleeding red lips moving silently—she chirped, "And see? I was right. I'm twenty bucks richer."

Afterward, we drove to Woodfield Mall. It seemed like all of Schaumburg High School was there, flitting and cutting loose beneath the artificial lights. It reminded me of that scene from *A Midsummer Night's Dream* where Puck and the other fairies cavort through the forest, feasting and frolicking and causing trouble. I waved to some girls from last semester's chem class, proud to be seen with Collin's arm around my shoulders. A couple. *The* couple. Like Hamlet and Ophelia, or Rosalind and Orlando.

Collin and Lily.

*Lovers eternal, side by side.*

At the food court, Drew begged me for money for a pretzel.

"Come on, Lily," he whined. "I'm broke and I'm starving."

*"Neither a borrower nor a lender be,"* I replied, taking a sip of my Diet Coke. "Guess you'll just have to wish for it."

Drew pulled the monkey paw out of his pocket, held it above his head and said dramatically, "O magic monkey paw, I wish for . . . Naw, forget it."

"What?" asked Collin. "Afraid it won't work?"

"Afraid to waste a wish." Drew grinned. "I mean, why ask for a lousy pretzel when I could ask to be a rock star or a gazillionaire? Besides, my generous, good-natured and, might I add, handsome big brother will buy me one, won't you, bro?"

"Only if you promise to wish me into being the greatest guitar player who ever lived."

"You got it," said Drew.

"Then your wish is my command." Collin handed Drew a five-dollar bill.

Drew scampered off to the pretzel line.

Alone, finally. Collin reached across the table and knit his fingers through mine. "If wishes really did come true, what would you wish for?" he asked.

I thought a moment. "I don't know. I have everything I want—a summer job, college next fall at Northwestern, you. *Especially* you."

His blue eyes warmed, and his beautiful mouth smiled. "Yeah, likewise," he said.

His words, so tender, freed my spirit. I wanted to shout to the sky, join the birds in their singing. Instead, I leaned forward and kissed him. And as always, I was instantly caught up in the scent of him, made dizzy by his closeness.

*Eternity was in our lips and eyes.*

"What'd I miss?" interrupted Drew, plopping down beside us.

Collin pulled away, and I felt a tiny pang of loss, as if some part of me had been misplaced.

"We were just talking about wishes," said Collin.

"Did you say wishes, or kisses?" joked Drew, his mouth full of pretzel.

"Hah, funny," I said.

"Besides a sense of humor," Collin asked him, "what else would you wish for?"

In reply, Drew wiped his greasy fingers down the front of his jeans, then pulled the monkey paw out of his pocket again. Winking at me, he once more held it above his head, and intoned, "O magic monkey paw, I wish for a 1972 Gran Torino with optional laser stripe and Magnum 500 wheels."

The lights in the mall flickered off, briefly plunging the place into shadowy darkness before snapping back on.

With a shout, Drew leaped to his feet, sending the

paw spinning to the floor. "It moved!" he cried, his eyes wide. "Its fingers wrapped around mine. I swear. I made the wish and that thing held my hand!"

"Get a grip," said Collin, patting Drew's shoulder. "That thing couldn't possibly have moved, doofus."

"It did," Drew said, his voice shaky. "I swear. It moved." He clutched my arm. "You believe me, don't you, Lily?"

His eyes were so intense, so sincere.

*Something wicked this way comes.*

"Let's go," I said, unable to keep an edge of urgency from creeping into my voice. "I think we should go."

"Whatever," Collin said, and cleared off the table while Drew bent to pick up the paw. He used his thumb and forefinger, as if he was picking up a pair of sweaty gym socks. Then he stuffed the paw back into his pocket.

Tight-lipped and tense, Drew followed us as we made our way through the mall and out into the parking lot.

"Just imagine it, bro," said Collin, trying to lighten the mood. "When we get home, I bet your Gran Torino will be parked right out front—red with black leather seats. And sitting right behind the three-spoke steering wheel, wearing a little orange fez, will be your chauffeur—a one-handed monkey!"

Drew tried on a laugh. "And *I* need a sense of humor?"

He stepped off the curb.

There was the blare of a horn . . . the squealing of

tires . . . Collin shouting, "Drew!" as he shoved his brother out of the way and then . . . a sickening thump.

So much blood. Everywhere. I ran to Collin, fell to the asphalt, held him close. His skin felt warm, but his eyes were frozen wide open, unmoving.

I whispered in his ear, "Wake up! Please, my heart, my love!" I shook him.

He grew heavy in my arms. And heavier.

"Oh God, oh God . . ."

A thread of blood trickled from the corner of his mouth—that beautiful, beautiful mouth. I wiped it away.

Then the sirens came.

And the numbness.

After the ambulance had taken Collin's body away, a policeman asked if I'd seen the car that had hit him.

"I'll always love him," I replied, my thoughts as trembling and detached as a leaf pausing in the air before the wind takes it. "I'll never love anyone else. Not as long as I live."

"Miss?" the policeman said. He laid a gentle hand on my arm. "Can you remember anything?"

I shook my head blankly.

*Blow, blow, thou winter wind . . .*

"I can." Drew stumbled forward, shock and horror etched on his face. "I saw it." His lips shaped his next words with effort. "It was a . . . a . . . Gran Torino—a 1972 Gran Torino with an . . . an optional laser stripe and . . . and Magnum 500 wheels."

*  *  *

I can recall only bits and pieces of Collin's funeral—
the stifling heat of the church; those endless, useless
prayers; the nauseating, overripe smell of lilies.

*O woe! O woeful, woeful, woeful day! Most lamentable
day, most woeful day, that ever, ever I did yet behold!*

What sticks most in my memory is the long line of
cars mournfully crawling the two miles to Mount Hope
Cemetery, where—sick and dizzy and clinging to Drew's
hand, feeling like I'd crumble if I let go—I stood beside
that hole cut deep into the ground.

Collin's grave.

*O day! O day! O day! O hateful day! Never was seen so
black a day as this. O woeful day! O woeful day!*

I wish I could say that my earlier numbness remained. It didn't. Now I felt *everything.* The loss of Collin
ate away at my bones, the pain creeping through my
veins. Everything—his picture in my wallet, his heart-
enclosed initials on my notebook covers—was a dreadful reminder that once he had existed, but now I had
lost him.

And so I slept. Afternoon. Night. Morning. It made
no difference. Sleep was my forgetting. My oblivion. My
only peace.

*To sleep, perchance to dream . . .*

Food forgotten, I grew gaunt, paper-skinned, my
hair dull and matted. I wanted nothing—nothing but to
be with him. I wanted to see him. I wanted to hold him.
I wanted him *alive.* I'd do anything.

*Anything!*

I sat up in bed, my heart swelling with the sudden joy of possibility.

It took six rings before Drew finally answered his phone.

"Hello?" His voice sounded thick and pinched.

"Unlock your back door," I said. "I'm coming over."

"Lily, is that you? What's going on?"

I couldn't waste precious time explaining. "Just do it. I'm leaving now."

Without bothering to change out of the nightgown I'd worn since returning from Collin's funeral a week earlier, I raced through the midnight-dark streets until I got to his house.

The sight of it was almost too much to bear, the memories flooding back, piercing me with longing: Collin and I cuddled together on his sofa, laughing, feeding each other popcorn, kissing . . . I refused to let my thoughts go any further.

It would be like that again, I told myself. It had to be!

Drew met me at the door. He looked ashen, his eyes swollen from too much crying.

"The paw!" I cried. "Do you still have it?"

Bewildered, he nodded. "I couldn't stand to look at it again. It's still under my bed where I threw it that afternoon."

I flung my arms around him. "Oh, Drew, why didn't we think of it before? We must have been crazy with grief not to think of it sooner."

"Think of what?"

"The other two wishes. You've only used one."

"Wasn't one enough? My brother . . ." His voice broke.

"We'll use another wish!" I cried. "Don't you see? *There are more things in heaven and earth than are dreamt of in your philosophy.* It's the paw! The magic paw! We'll wish Collin alive!"

Drew shook his head. "You're not thinking straight, Lily. People don't come back from the dead."

I wouldn't listen. Instead, I pushed past him into the house, hurried up the stairs to his bedroom.

Drew followed me, flipped on his light. I glanced around. His once car-covered walls were bare, the posters all gone. I fell to my knees, rummaged around in the mess of dirty socks and half-empty Doritos bags under his bed until my fingers found the paw. I pulled it out triumphantly, waved it at Drew.

"Hurry!" I cried. "Take it and make a wish."

Drew gripped my shoulders. "Come on, Lily. There's no such thing as a magic monkey paw." He looked away, and his voice dropped to barely a whisper. "It was just our imagination, that's all. A coincidence."

"You don't believe that," I said.

"Yes, I do."

He was lying. He believed in the monkey paw's magic as much as I did. So why wouldn't he make a wish? Why wouldn't he bring Collin back?

I knew what I was about to say was cruel, but I didn't care.

"You owe him this wish, Drew. Your first wish—your selfish first wish—killed him. So you can either bring him back alive, or live with his blood on your hands. It's your choice."

"No," he groaned.

"Wish," I urged.

He hesitated.

*"Wish!"*

His expression turned fierce then, belligerent. Raising the paw above his head, he cried, "I wish Collin was alive again!"

Outside, the world fell silent, as if muffled by some giant hand.

Inside, the paw fell to the floor, and Drew's fierce expression faded. Slumping onto the floor, he moaned, "No, no, no, no."

"He'll come to me now!" I shrieked gleefully. "I know it. He's rushing to me already."

I hurried to the window and looked out.

*Love goes toward love.*

"No, no, no, no." Behind me, Drew was still moaning.

"He'll come. I can feel it. Feel *him*. We just have to be patient." In my madness to hold Collin again, I babbled. "The cemetery is two miles away. It will take some time. But the wish worked. It worked!"

I had already turned back to the window, searching

the street for Collin—my beautiful, beloved Collin—when Drew said, "I know he'll come. That's what scares me."

"Scares you? He's your brother."

Drew stood. Gripping my shoulders, he turned me to face him. "Think, Lily. He's been dead for days— embalmed, buried, sealed in a box in the ground for *seven whole days*."

"No," I said. "He wouldn't come back like that. That's not what you wished for. You wished for him to be alive like he was before."

"Those who interfere with their fate only meet great sorrow," said Drew, quoting from Mrs. Alvarez's story. "Don't you get it? The wishes always go bad."

There was a soft knock on the back door.

I stood motionless, holding my breath, barely able to hope.

The knock sounded again.

"It's Collin!" I cried. "It's my heart!"

I took two steps before Drew caught my arm and held me tightly. "What are you going to do?"

"I'm going to answer the door. Let me go, it's my Collin!"

Breaking free, I plunged down the dark staircase.

Drew was behind me, holding me back, frantic. "Don't let it in," he pleaded. "For God's sake, Lily. Can't you smell it?"

"Smell what?" I squirmed in his grip.

"Death," sobbed Drew. "Wet earth and decay. You can't let it in. I won't let you." He locked his arms around my waist and began dragging me back up the stairs to his bedroom, his skinny body stronger than I'd ever imagined.

For a moment, I hesitated, saw the certainty and determination in Drew's eyes. Was he right?

*O, that way madness lies . . .*

"No!"

I fought him. I kicked and thrashed.

There was another knock at the door. More insistent this time. Then another. And another.

My beloved was there, within my reach, if only—

I sank my teeth into Drew's upper arm. I felt his flesh give way, tasted the iron tinge of his blood.

He screamed, pushed me away. For one second, I tottered on the edge of the stairs, arms whirling, frantically trying to gain my balance. I made a wild clutch at the handrail. Then I was cartwheeling down the stairs, rolling over and over until I hit bottom. I felt a searing, sharp pain, my neck giving way with a loud *snap!* Then I was floating, floating away . . .

Drew stood at the top of the stairs, anguished tears streaming down his face, the monkey paw held high above his head. He had one last wish.

I heard another knock on the back door.

I felt my life slipping away.

*One last wish, Drew. Save me!*

His lips moved. "I wish my brother dead again."

"Noooooo!"

The knocking stopped.

So, too, did my time on earth.

Mike felt a wave of sympathy so strong and spontaneous that it made his eyes sting. He blinked back the tears. The last thing he wanted to do was burst out crying in front of a bunch of kids—even dead ones. Still, that kind of loss—how could she endure it? Keeping his head down, he breathed slowly and deliberately.

It was Blanche who put into words what he was feeling. "Wretchedly tragic," she said with a sorrowful shake of her head, "to have not only lost your life, but your love as well."

"Oh, but I didn't lose *love*," corrected Lily. "Real love, like mine and Collin's, has no final act." She smiled. "And you know what else? Collin is out there, loving me and waiting for me. We'll be together again. I know it." She looked toward the sky, her eyes glowing.

> *"Doubt thou the stars are fire,*
> *Doubt that the sun doth move;*
> *Doubt truth to be a liar;*
> *But never doubt I love."*

Mike followed the direction of her gaze, half-expecting Collin's ghost to float down from the sky. But all he saw was the polished-bone moon and a sprinkling of fading stars.

"It's not just love that lives forever," said a new voice.

Mike turned to find a boy in a pair of jeans and a T-shirt standing beside a simple granite stone.

"You see this grave with my name on it?" the boy said, pointing. "It's empty . . . well, almost empty. If you were to dig down through the tree roots and earthworms, you'd find a casket and not much else. There *is* one thing buried down there, though."

"What's that?" asked Mike.

"A chrome hood ornament. It was the only thing my folks were left with . . . *afterward*. All those rescue workers. The salvage crew. And all they ever found was that rotten hood ornament. Weird, huh?"

Mike and the others nodded.

"Even weirder was Mom and Dad's decision to bury it in my place, give it a funeral. I like to think Kev convinced them to do that, that he saw a way to be rid of the cursed thing and memorialize me at the same time. But I'll never know for sure. All I know is that they nestled the ornament into the tailored red crepe of the Concord Casket Company's Autumn Oak Special and buried it.

"Six feet down.

"Sealed for all eternity from leakage and rust.

"And you know what else?

"I bet . . . no, I *know* it's glowing down there in the pitch-blackness of my grave. Can't you feel it?

"Glowing red.

"And seething mad.

"Evil that never dies . . ."

# RICH

## 1965–1981

M Y BEST FRIEND, KEV, wasn't a crazy driver. You need to know that right up front. On the day it all began, his license was only two weeks old, and he was being even more cautious and uptight than usual.

Basically, this meant he was a total basket case.

"Tell me again," Kev said nervously as we exited onto I-94 and headed east toward Indiana. "Why are we doing this?" Both his hands clenched the steering wheel, his white knuckles positioned at ten and two just like we'd learned in driver's ed.

"Because it's an adventure, man," I replied, trying as usual to pump up his enthusiasm. "Because we've got nothing better to do. Because"—I patted the car seat—"the grandpa-mobile deserves something a little more bangin' than Papa Smurf."

Earlier that summer, Kev's folks had given him the

keys to his grandfather's old Chrysler Newport, a puke-beige four-door complete with rooftop luggage rack and bench seats. Honest, bench seats! They'd even come with those beaded seat covers tied over them. You know, the kind that are supposed to massage your back while you're driving? Anyway, the first thing Kev did was yank out those covers. Underneath, the upholstery was pockmarked with cigarette burns, and tufts of padding poked up through the holes. Until he could find something better, he'd covered it all up with a *Smurfs* beach towel he'd taken from his mom's linen closet.

"Really? You couldn't have just grabbed a plain brown one?" I'd said the first time I'd planted my butt on that sprawling village of blue cottages. Shuddering, I'd inched closer to the door so I wouldn't have to sit on Papa Smurf's face. Talk about creepy!

Kev gulped. "I didn't want to take anything too nice. My mom might have gotten mad."

I snorted. Like cookie-baking Mrs. Longo was going to go nuclear over a Kmart brand bath towel, right? But that was classic Kev. He maneuvered through his life as timidly as he drove his car, his eyes constantly searching the horizon for phantom accidents, his foot always hovering above the brake pedal.

I patted the crazy towel, reminding him of our errand. "Really, man," I said. "If you go back to school next week sporting *this,* nothing can save you, not even me."

I'd been saving Kev ever since that day way back in

eighth grade when he'd walked into the lunchroom of Richard J. Daley Junior High School. Half the size of the other guys and skinny as a Twizzler, he stood there—the new kid—one hand picking nervously at a scab on his pointy chin, the other clutching the handle of his *Battlestar Galactica* lunch box. He scanned the room, looking for a place to sit down.

"Look what the cat dragged in," drawled the ever-original Doug Buell. "A munchkin!"

A couple of the guys at my table snickered.

Encouraged, Buell went on, "Hey, runt, where'd you get that lunch box? From Babies 'R' Us?"

"Come on," I said, seeing Kev's face redden. "Leave him alone."

But Buell figured he was on a roll. He swaggered over to Kev. "So this is what Oscar looks like out of his trash can. Man, that's uh-uh-uh-gly!"

Kev kind of ducked into himself, like a turtle into its shell.

And I pushed up from the table. I wasn't trying to be a hero or anything, but when you've got three little sisters at home, you can't help developing a soft spot for the weak and defenseless.

I stepped toward Buell. "Chill out, Doug." I poked him in the forehead with my finger.

He poked me back.

I shoved him in the chest.

He shoved me back.

I punched him in the shoulder. Twice. Hard. "Leave

him alone," I repeated. Maybe it was the seriousness of my tone, or the fact that none of the other guys were laughing anymore, or maybe the timer on his tiny attention span had gone off. Whatever the reason, Buell backed down. But not without a parting shot. "Guess you've found a member of your own species, huh, Grabowski?"

I shrugged. "If you mean the *human* species, then I guess so," I replied. I headed back to the table, Kev in tow.

I'd been towing him ever since.

The green-and-white exit marker came up on our left. Kev put on his signal and conscientiously checked his rearview mirror. Then, puttering along at ten miles below the speed limit, we drove down Cline Avenue to Columbus and made a right into a car wasteland bogusly called Darryl's Auto Salvage. I say bogus, because Darryl's was nothing but twelve acres of crushed and rusted car remains surrounded by a five-foot-high corrugated tin fence. The place blended in real good with the rest of the junk that lined the southern lip of Lake Michigan— oil refineries, steel mills, pawnshops.

Kev pulled onto a graveled patch that looked like a parking area and turned off the car's engine. "I don't think we're going to find any seat covers here."

I figured he was right. Still, we'd just braved the Chicago traffic, driven the forty miles from Tinley Park. "Let's check it out," I said.

We wound our way through the maze of scrap metal

and car parts. Around one curve we found a slip-sliding mountain of hubcaps; around another was a precariously balanced tower of balding tires. I freed a front spoiler from a tangle of belts and hoses, kicked at an oozing battery. That's when I saw the hood ornament, its flawless chrome glowing bright against the rusting skeleton of a Packard hearse.

Kev saw it, too, and he gave a little gasp. Walking over with exaggerated casualness, he picked it up. I know it's weird, but for a second he looked like he was holding a ball of fire, like the thing might actually scorch his hands. Its glow lit up his face, spotlighting the smile forming on his lips. He didn't have to say a word. I knew he wanted it.

The ornament was shaped like a stallion rearing up in a fighting stance—neck arched, muscles taut, front hooves beating the empty air. On its ferocious face, its nostrils flared, and its eyes—red stones sunk deep into the metal—flashed with anger. Two nubs, like tiny horns, sprouted from its forehead. And its chrome lips, curled back in the heat of battle, revealed teeth that were not really teeth, but fangs. Razor-sharp like a wolf's, not a horse's.

What's that about? I wondered.

Kev glanced at the price tag taped to its bottom.

"Ten bucks," he said. He pulled out his billfold, counted his money, sighed. "I don't suppose—"

I shook my head. "Sorry, man, I'm busted."

"Then there's only one thing to do," said Kev. He tucked the ornament under his shirt.

"No way!" I gasped. *"You're* going to *steal* it? *You?"*

I couldn't believe it. Not Kev. Not the guy who made his bed every morning, who returned his library books on time, who came to a complete, three-second stop at every stop sign!

"You're kidding, right?" I said.

But I knew he wasn't. Crossing his bony arms over the conspicuous lump under his shirt, he sidled toward the parking lot. "Are you coming, or what?" he asked.

Licking my lips, which were suddenly dry, I glanced over at the shack that served as the junkyard's office. Through its one grimy window, I could see Darryl—a concrete block of a guy—talking on the phone. His face had the look of a pit bull. He leaned forward to peer at us through the streaked glass.

"This is *not* a good idea," I hissed.

But Kev just kept going. Bent over, pressing the ornament to his belly, he speed-walked toward the gap in the corrugated fence and out into the parking lot. Not exactly nonchalant.

The office door popped open, and Darryl's beefy shape filled the frame. "Hey," he shouted, "what're you kids up to?"

"N-n-not a thing," I stammered, trying to keep my cool. Whirling, I took off after Kev.

He was already in the Chrysler, the motor running. "Quick, get in," he said.

As I flung myself into the passenger seat, Kev put it into gear. Even though he was driving the getaway car, he signaled before turning left onto Cline Avenue.

"This is no time to drive like an old man!" I shouted. "Put the pedal to the metal!"

He inched the grandpa-mobile up to the speed limit.

I caught my breath, let a few miles pass before turning to Kev. "What was that about? We could have gotten our friggin' butts flattened back there," I told him, although *friggin'* and *butt* weren't exactly the words I used. "And all for that . . . that piss-ugly piece of metal." I looked down at the ornament lying on the seat between us.

"I couldn't leave it, Rich," said Kev, his eyes kind of glazing over for a second. "I don't know why, but I *had* to take it. It was like it wanted me to . . . like it *insisted.*"

"It insisted you *steal* it?" I snorted.

"I know it doesn't make any sense, but it's the truth. I—"

He stopped, as if something had interrupted his thoughts. Pulling over to the side of the road and triple-checking to make sure the car's blinkers were on, he grabbed the ornament and climbed out of the car.

"Now what?" I said.

"I just need a minute." He walked around to the front of the grandpa-mobile and set the ornament on its hood. The thing looked both silly *and* spooky, like one of those fake tombstones people put in their front yards at Halloween. For a second, Kev just ran his hands over the ornament's glinting chrome. Then, after pawing around in the car's backseat for a roll of duct tape and a wire coat hanger, he started jerry-rigging it to the car.

I got out, too. "Can't you at least wait until we get home?" I asked. I was still worried about Darryl.

Kev shook his head. "It has to go on now."

"How come?"

"It just does."

I persisted. "What's the big hurry?"

Kev whirled, face flushed, sweaty hair flopping. "Because I want to put it on now, Rich. Okay? It has to go on right *now!*"

I raised my hands in mock surrender. "Hey, defib, okay? You stole it, so I guess you can do whatever you want with it. But it's going to be hard not to say 'I told you so' when it goes flying on the expressway."

Kev slapped another piece of duct tape around the base of the thing, gave it a test wiggle. "It's not going to fall off. It's on good and tight."

I doubted it. Kev's mechanical abilities rated right up there with his social skills—meaning they were practically zilch. Three different times he'd tried to fix the grandpa-mobile's passenger seat belt—a matter of simply tightening the retractable spool—and three different times he'd failed. The belt was still useless, all thirteen feet of it hanging out like a dog's tongue on a hot summer's day.

I climbed into the car and sat on that lame beach towel.

Kev slid behind the wheel. But he didn't start the engine right away. Instead, he sat gazing through the windshield at the shimmering stallion. "Want to hear something strange, Rich?" he finally said. "I really like seeing that hood ornament out there. It makes me feel, I don't know, like Clark Kent bursting out of a phone booth or something. Kind of invincible, like nothing and no one can touch me."

From then on, things were pretty normal until we got back into the city. I pushed Cheap Trick into the cassette deck, then banged along on the dashboard while Kev clutched the steering wheel and navigated rush-hour traffic. But as the city's skyline rose into view, something came over Kev. He was staring straight ahead, his eyes wide despite the blinding glare ricocheting off the hood ornament.

"Earth to Kev," I called.

That's when the wildness crept into his face.

"Kev?" I asked. "You okay?"

Kev answered by smashing down the accelerator. The car leaped forward.

"Holy crap!" I cried as the grandpa-mobile registered speeds you can bet it'd never reached before—

ninety . . . ninety-five . . . a hundred miles per hour! "What's the matter with you? Slow down!"

Kev yanked the car across three lanes of traffic. Brake lights flashed. Horns blasted. "Woo-hoo!" he hollered, as if he was riding one of the roller coasters at Great America. He sped up, slipping behind a gravel truck.

"Slow down! Slow down!" I cried as the truck's back end loomed, filling the windshield. I braced for the impact, sure we were going to die in a fiery crash.

Kev swerved out of the lane without even checking his side mirror, barely missing a blue Chevette. The guy driving lay on his horn. Kev just laughed and tore away, careening through the traffic like a psycho.

My stomach lurched and my armpits turned to puddles. "Stop it! Slow down!"

He grinned at me like a jack-o'-lantern. "I told you, Rich. I'm invincible, man. In-friggin'-vincible!" He tilted back his head and howled like a wolf.

Then he gave the accelerator another punch, and the Chrysler responded like a rocket. Veering crazily onto the shoulder, he took the 159th Street exit ramp so fast I bounced out of my seat. Outside, the familiar sights of Tinley Park swept past in a blur of color and speed. Just minutes later, Kev wheeled the car into my driveway, coming to a squealing, slantways stop.

"Are you crazy?" I gasped, clawing open the passenger door and stumbling out onto the driveway. "You could have killed us both!"

"But I didn't," said Kev, his chest still heaving from his adrenaline rush. "That was some ride, huh?"

It was all I could do not to knock his teeth down his throat. Kicking the car door shut, I huffed toward the house.

"Hey," he called after me. "What's your problem?"

I didn't even look back. I just kept walking.

I steered clear of Kev for the next week or so. Sure, I was still plenty mad, but I was scared, too. And not just by his driving. No, something else had frightened me. It was the look on his face as he'd clenched that steering wheel. Wild. Uncontrolled. His eyes glinting like those on that crazy chrome horse he'd strapped to his hood.

Then on the Saturday before school started, he pulled up in front of my house.

"Hey," he said. He got out of the Chrysler and strolled up the driveway to where I was tinkering under the hood of my beater, a '72 Ford Pinto I'd dumped my entire life savings into—all five hundred bucks of it. "Looks like she's coming along." Leaning down, he tapped the new running lights I'd just installed. "Looks good."

I knew this was Kev's way of making up, that his complimenting my wreck of a car was the closest I'd ever get to an apology. I accepted it.

Pulling my head out from under the hood, I took a closer look at him. Jeez, he looked like crap! His eyes were sunken, and he'd lost weight. His T-shirt hung on him like wet laundry, and his belt—cinched on the last hole—barely held up his baggy jeans.

"What have you been up to?" I asked, wondering if he'd been sick.

"Driving," he said. "I've been driving."

Just the word seemed to trigger a change in him.

"There's nothing like driving, Rich," he went on, and even though his face looked hungry, his voice sounded slack, as if he was reciting some dull poem from lit class. "It fills your mind, and all you can think of is going fast, going far, *getting there.*"

He wasn't making any sense. "Getting where?"

"Wherever the roads take me—to the city, to Mexico, to the moon. It doesn't matter just as long as I'm driving."

He looked away for a moment, and when he looked back his face had lost its wildness. In its place was a sad, thoughtful expression. "I should go."

"What's your hurry?" I said. "You just got here."

"I know, but . . ." He stumbled around for an excuse before adding, "I've got to be somewhere."

"Where?"

Kev didn't answer. He just started down the driveway toward his car.

I trailed after him. "Listen, man, are you okay? Do you need—"

I couldn't finish my sentence. The grandpa-mobile! It was as changed as Kev. A spiderweb of cracks spread across the left side of the windshield. The right rear bumper was caved in. And the puke-beige paint blistered and bubbled in places as if he had driven it through a furnace. The car was ruined . . . well, *almost*. The hood ornament still glowed shiny and bright.

When he opened the driver's door, a hot billow of air puffed out. It stank of burned matches and something else I didn't recognize. Papa Smurf was singed a dull brown.

"What's this all about, man?" I asked. "What happened?"

"Driving happened," he answered. Sliding in behind the steering wheel, he turned the key.

The Chrysler's motor revved, and I swear I saw smoke—*real* smoke—puff from the stallion's flaring nostrils.

Kev leaned out the window then, and his eyes met mine. "There are back roads out there, Rich. Lonely, forgotten roads leading to places no one's ever gone, places that can't be found on any map."

"What do you mean?"

The car revved again, eager and impatient. The hood ornament seemed to glow even brighter, its red eyes flashing.

"It's time to go," Kev said. Putting the car in gear, he roared away.

I stood there, looking down the empty street.

*Back roads . . . places that can't be found on any map.*

Worry began to eat at me.

"Where have you been going, Kev?" I said to no one. "Where have you been going?"

The next afternoon, I took a stroll over to Kev's house. The grandpa-mobile was in the driveway. It was splattered with something wet and slippery that reminded me of the insides of the fetal pigs we'd dissected last year in biology. In places, the splatters were chunkier, fleshier. Picking up a stick, I poked at an especially big chunk. It oozed pus green.

I jumped back, startled and disgusted, and flung the stick away. With a shudder, I wiped my hand on my jeans. I saw black smoke seeping from beneath the hood, giving off that same acrid burned-match stench I'd smelled coming from the front seat yesterday. The car's paint was bubbled over most of the fenders and hood, and along the wheel wells black scorch marks angled backward.

Behind me the screen door slammed.

I turned.

Somehow, Kev looked even thinner than yesterday—his dark eyes hollow, his skin pulled tight over his skull. He shuffled toward me, car keys in his hand.

"What's the deal, Kev?" I was shaken and needed answers.

"I told you. I've been driving."

I glanced back at the car. On the hood, the stallion's red eyes began to glow orange, like hot coals. It was as if a fire was burning *inside* the ornament, as if I was looking through the window of a furnace.

It all became clear to me. "It's the hood ornament, isn't it? It has some sort of power over you."

His laugh sounded hollow. "It's led me on amazing adventures, Rich, taken me to incredible places."

"Have you lost your mind?" I grabbed his shoulders and shook him. "Come on, Kev. Walk away from it. Just walk away."

"You don't get it! I'm different now," he said. He stepped around me and got into the car.

"This isn't you!" I shouted. "Don't you see? It's that . . . that . . . thing!" I grabbed it, to rip it from the car's hood. It was searing hot, frying the skin on my palms like bacon. I jumped back, waving my throbbing hands, blowing on my blistered fingertips.

Kev started the engine.

"Stop!" I cried.

"I can't, Rich," he said. "Don't you see? I have to drive."

I yanked open the passenger door and grabbed wildly for the keys. Kev batted me away, and in that second, the car bolted backward, flinging me headfirst into the space between the seat and the glove compartment. With a screech, the car roared down the road, weaving and careening like a rodeo horse, like it was trying to toss me out. And I would have fallen out, too, if not for the length of broken seat belt coiled on the floor. I grabbed it, clung to it, used it to steady myself on the front seat.

"Get out!" shouted Kev. "Get out while you still can!" Taking a hand off the steering wheel, he shoved me hard.

I swung toward the still-open door, gripping the seat belt, feeling a rush of wind and pavement inches from my face. The car made a hard turn and the force pulled me back in. I grasped the door and yanked it shut.

The locks clamped down with a snap that sounded like a gunshot.

"No, no, no!" Kev moaned beside me. He was wrestling with the steering wheel, trying to gain some control. "This is all wrong. You shouldn't be here. It was supposed to be just me—just me and *it*."

Through the windshield I could see the stallion. Chrome legs pumping, hooves pounding. The thing was alive!

Fear coiled inside me, thick and suffocating.

"Slam on the brakes!" I shouted.

"Don't you get it?" cried Kev. "There's nothing we can do—nothing but go along for the ride."

Outside the window, our neighborhood melted into a blur. In seconds—yes, seconds—we were on I-94, leaving the city. I turned in my seat to look out the back window as Chicago's skyline winked goodbye.

And then we were barreling along roads I'd never known existed, country roads that were abandoned and forlorn, snaking through tangled marshes and treeless fields. Once we shot across an expanse of bloodred water on a rickety suspension bridge, and I covered my eyes, sure we would plummet to our deaths. Instead we dropped into the dark, wet throat of a tunnel that spiraled down into complete darkness. I couldn't see a thing, only sense the hurtling speed, feel the car heating up. I screamed just to let myself know I was still there. Still in the car. Still alive.

Kev's voice came to me through the blackness. "Brimstone. That smell is brimstone."

It was the same sulfury, burned-match smell that had invaded me in Kev's driveway, only this time it was all over me. Coating my skin. Creeping into my lungs. The stench burned my nostrils, seared my throat, made my eyes stream.

"I'm so sorry, Rich," said Kev. "You weren't supposed to come along on this trip."

We shot out of the tunnel into a tangled forest. As we hurtled along the narrow dirt road, the trees scratched and clawed at the car, and an especially big oak limb slammed into the passenger window, shattering the glass. I shrieked as the Chrysler skittered off the road and into the woods, plowing through barbed grasses and bushes with thorns the size of kitchen knives. Snakelike vines writhed and knotted, while black toadstools dripped yellow poison onto the forest floor. All around us the air was thick with black flies the size of my fist.

We burst out of the woods at the top of a tall sand dune, and I recognized where we were. I knew this place. It was Mount Baldy, one of the tallest dunes on Lake Michigan. Only it wasn't. It was like everything was backward, as if I was looking at it from the wrong side.

The Chrysler stopped at the very top of the dune. It idled, catching its breath.

Spread out before us as far as the eye could see was water—a boiling black witches' cauldron of water. It stretched to the horizon, where red bolts of lightning flashed and angry storm clouds swirled. The air grew hot, furnace hot, so hot that tiny burning cinders began to fall from the sky like rain. They hissed and sizzled on the sand, the waves, the roof of the car.

*A firestorm. It's a firestorm.*

Overhead, thunder rumbled.

The car revved its motor in eager answer.

I felt the back wheels spin in the sand, searching for traction. On the hood, the stallion's powerful front hooves pawed the fiery air.

I didn't have time to think it through. I still had the seat belt in my hand. I saw the shattered passenger window. I seized my chance—my *only* chance.

"There's no use fighting," Kev said hopelessly as I knotted the strap around my waist and began to crawl out the window. "You can't win."

"I can try!" I shouted.

I was hanging halfway out when the car leaped forward, propelling me the rest of the way through the window. Jagged shards of glass raked across my legs as I was flung backward like a tethered kite, slamming onto the car's trunk.

I crouched there a moment, caught my breath, the cinders burning tiny holes in my shirt, my jeans, my skin. Then, with all my might, I gripped the luggage rack. Fighting the searing heat of its metal, I heaved myself up and over the roof. The fiery wind screamed in my ears. The heated sand pelted my skin like buckshot. The car hit the beach, charging toward the water's edge. I had just seconds left. Eyes squeezed shut, I let myself roll down the windshield and across the hood. As I did, I felt patches of my skin peel away from my face and arms, sizzling like hamburgers on a grill.

The seat belt held, pulled me up short, my head dangling between the car's headlights. Somehow I managed to right myself, brace my feet against the front grille and grasp the white-hot hood ornament. Steam rose from my hands, and the burned-meat stench of charred flesh—*my flesh*—savaged my nose. But I was beyond caring, beyond pain. I wrenched the monstrous ornament from the hood.

I struggled to hold it as the stallion kicked and bucked furiously in my charred hands. Arching its neck, it turned and sank its fanglike teeth into my thumb, its red eyes wide and maniacal.

"*You* can go to the devil!" I screamed at the top of my lungs. And just as the Chrysler reached the water's edge, I flung the ornament. I heaved it with all my might. It flew through the thick heat, legs flailing, eyes blazing. Out of the roiling water rose a hungry wave. It snatched the ornament in midair. There came a loud hiss and a spout of red steam, and then the ornament was gone, devoured by the lake.

And in that instant, everything changed. Suddenly, I was looking at the beach and Mount Baldy as I'd always known them. The water was blue again, cold instead of boiling. A cool breeze lifted off the waves. I turned my blistered face, took a deep breath.

"The lake!" Kev hollered, and panic filled his voice. "The lake! We're sinking!"

We were still in the water, the car's hot metal sizzling as we sank. Already the water was up to the bumpers, and it was rising quickly.

"Kev!" I shouted as I wrestled with the knot around my waist. "Get out of there!"

I could see him through the windshield—his eyes clear—the old Kev I'd always known. Rolling down his window, he splashed into the water and dog-paddled clumsily toward me.

"Get going! Get help!" I panted, gesturing toward the beach. "I'm right behind you." I tore frantically at the seat belt, but it was no use. My ruined fingers couldn't work the knot. The water was deep now. Even though I was kneeling on the hood, the waves splashed around my waist.

"B-but . . . ," sputtered Kev.

"Get going!" I shouted.

I watched him paddle toward shore as the water crept up my chest. The knot was too tight, the seat belt too strong. I wasn't going to escape. But Kev would. I watched him stumble, coughing and struggling, onto the beach, calling for help.

And then, just as the lake closed over my head, I saw it, glinting in the afternoon sun just where Kev had emerged . . . a chrome stallion bucking in the surf.

For several long seconds, Mike stared down at Rich's grave. Was it his imagination, or could he actually feel a vibration from below, something malevolent radiating up through the dirt?

Mike jumped away and hurried back to Carol Anne's grave. "Creepy," he said with a shudder, "that thing still down there . . . waiting."

"We're all waiting for something, even him," said Scott, jerking his head in the direction of a willow tree.

Almost completely hidden behind the tree's draping branches, a rail-thin, long-haired figure sat, silent and unmoving. The figure's arms were folded across his chest, and his white hands—sickly white hands that Mike bet had never seen the sun even in life—gleamed in the bone-glow of the moon. Although his face was turned away, Mike could tell that the ghost was fixated on some nameless object in the distance, his expressionless eyes wide and staring.

"Hey, mutton head!" shouted Johnnie. "Whatcha got to say for yourself?"

"Shhh," said Mike, suddenly panicked. "Let's not . . . um . . . disturb him."

"But, Mike, everybody needs to tell their story, remember?" said Gina.

"Yeah," Mike said reluctantly. He sensed that he didn't want to hear this one, didn't want to listen to any tale this ghost might have to tell. "I remember."

"C'mon, kid," Johnnie hollered again. "Spit it out."

A spasm shook the ghost, as if he'd felt a sudden chill. Shambling to his feet, he shuffled forward. His cheeks were thin to hollowness, his mouth a tortured line. He looked around at the others before settling those strange, blank eyes on Mike. And then he began to speak.

# EDGAR

## 1853–1870

THE WALLPAPER WAS ALIVE.

Its flocked-velvet pattern of uncertain curves and twisting angles slithered across the guest room walls in varying hues of reds—here a lurid scarlet, there a pale vermilion, over by the window a sickly, faded pink, the color of a dying rose. It was hideous. Yet I could not look away. It provoked me. Commanded me to trace its tortuous pattern hour upon hour.

There was, I observed, a spot in the pattern that swirled in on itself, lolling like a broken neck. If I turned my head just so, the broken neck dissolved into a set of glowering red eyes. They accused me, those eyes. Always.

*How dare the wallpaper look at me that way!*

There was another place just above the bedstead where two strips of the paper refused to line up evenly. The unmatched pattern formed a slit of a mouth, and in that mouth a line of clenched white teeth.

The vision of that ghastly mouth jerked me from my pondering so suddenly that I felt like a hooked fish. One moment I was peacefully suspended in the murky depths of my musings, the next I was gasping on the shores of consciousness. And it was all because of the wallpaper.

Oh, how I despised that wallpaper!

How its mocking images drove me to fury!

Sometimes, after waking, I wept. Other times, I slammed my fists into the wallpaper as if trying to beat it into a velvet pulp.

"What is happening to me?" I asked myself after one such incident. I resolved never to enter the guest bedroom again.

For a few days I stood by this pledge. And still, those twisting bloodred patterns dwelt in my mind as the glass paperweight once did; as the brass knobs had done before it. And just as with those other objects, there were things about that wallpaper that nobody knew but me.

*Secret things.*

I was not always like that, tortured and alone. Once upon a time, I had a home. A family. But I also had the ponderings.

I have *always* had the ponderings.

I was born with them as surely as I was born with heart, liver and lungs. Slit open my belly, I believed, and you would find them there, tangled among the blood and viscera. Passed down from previous generations, folded into my very soul, the ponderings were a part of me.

I was three years old the first time I was taken by one. I remember standing in the nursery, holding a colored building block in my pudgy hand. Blue it was, a rectangle of wood. I held it, and all of a sudden, I felt weightless. The blood in my head swirled, and the hand holding the block began to tingle. For one moment I felt like a tea-kettle about to whistle.

Then the outside world simply slipped away. I was no longer aware of the Turkish carpet beneath my feet, or of my other toys, or even of my nursemaid rocking quietly in the corner. The blue block commanded my full atten-tion. All my focus. Every corner of my mind. I turned the toy over. I could make out the tiny lines of the wood's grain, smell its faint piney odor, sense the nearly invisi-ble strokes of the paintbrush. I dwelt on the block's heft. I lingered on its shape. And in my mind's eye, I could change it. Alter it. I saw the block miraculously stretch-ing, expanding into toy houses and streets, then en-larging into real houses, real streets, then into schools, shops, cities, entire nations all made of my rectangular blue block. I became one with the block—my mood, my thoughts, everything. I was the block. The block was I.

I awakened from this state—surfaced as if from a pool—sweating and shivering in my crib. Mother and Fa-ther were peering down at me with pinched faces while the nursemaid held a cold compress to my forehead.

"His eyes are open!" Mother cried.

Another face joined theirs, gray-bearded and wearing spectacles. Dr. Marquis pressed a stethoscope to my chest. "How do you feel, little fellow?" he said. "You've been away for hours."

Away? Whatever did he mean by *away*? I blinked. I felt as if I had just awoken from a very confused, yet very exciting dream.

"I'm thirsty," I said.

While the nursemaid lifted my head and touched a glass of water to my lips, my parents and the doctor huddled together by the door. I strained my ears to hear, catching words I did not understand, like *monomania* and *madness.*

"Madness?" gasped Mother.

"Utter nonsense," hissed Father. Even though I could not see his face, I could tell he was clenching his teeth the way he always did when he was angry.

Mother cringed. "Charles," she began, her voice fluttering nervously. She reached out tentatively, laid a timid hand on his arm.

He shoved it away. "No one in the Allerton family has ever been given to such weakness, either in body *or* in mind."

"But if the doctor thinks poor little Edgar is ill, perhaps it would be best—"

Father exploded. "Edgar is *not* ill, I say!"

Mother seemed to collapse inward. "Yes, Charles," she hastily agreed. "You're right, of course. As always."

Father turned on Dr. Marquis, his white teeth

gnashing with rage. "No one must hear of this . . . this episode," he growled. "I cannot tolerate gossip about myself or my family. Do you understand me? No one must hear of this. No one!"

Dr. Marquis placed a bracing hand on Father's shoulder. "And no one *will* hear of it, sir, I can assure you. Besides, I am not suggesting that Edgar is permanently mad. No, in my opinion this is a singular incident, brought on by too few naps, perhaps, or too many rich foods. There is no reason to believe that little Edgar will experience another such episode."

He was wrong, of course. The doctors were always wrong. As I grew older, my ponderings (as I came to call them) grew stronger, more frequent and intense. For an entire evening my attention could be riveted by a spider's web. I could lose a whole day contemplating a flower petal that had fallen onto the carpet.

And as these episodes became more pronounced, I could feel Father hardening toward me. No longer did he look across the dining table with paternal pride, or talk of the day when I would take over the family pork-packing business. Each of my ponderings was yet another brick in the wall that was growing between us.

"What would my business associates say if they knew I had sired such a feeble-minded son!" growled Father to Mother one afternoon.

I had been playing on the parlor floor with my tin

soldiers—the ones I had received just a week earlier for my eleventh birthday—when I had slipped away, pondering the fringe at the carpet's edge. By the time I returned to myself minutes later, Father was glaring, his hard white teeth clenched.

"Why, the lower classes have a better grasp of reality than he does," he raged on.

By "lower classes," I knew he meant the men who worked for him—Irish and German immigrants mostly, who spent fourteen hours a day covered in a mixture of animal grease and blood, all for the handful of pennies Father paid them; men whose families shivered in rotting pine shanties surrounded by slime and disease while we resided in our thirty-room mansion with its elegant mansard roof and sprawling green lawn.

"Have I worked myself to the bone merely to hand it all over to a lunatic son?" He ground his teeth. "I tell you, Adele, I can hardly stand to look at him."

"He'll outgrow it." Mother's voice quavered. "The doctors have promised he'll outgrow it."

"He had better," Father said with a cold finality.

There was a brisk knock at the parlor door then, and our housekeeper, Mrs. Kolin, entered with a message for Father.

"It's from Cyrus McCormick!" he exclaimed after reading the note. "He is coming *here* tomorrow morning to discuss business." Gone was the anger of moments before. Now Father looked more buoyant and elated than

I had ever seen him. "Do you know what an honor it is to receive a call from such a man as Mr. McCormick? Do you?" He whirled on Mother. "Everything must be arranged perfectly, do you understand, Adele? The flowers, the luncheon . . ."

"Oh, yes, Charles," Mother said brightly, obediently. "I will see to it all."

From the carpet, I smiled at Father's happy mood.

His eyes fell on me, and the pleasure drained from his face. "And for Heaven's sake, Adele, keep *him* out of sight."

Mother tensed. She nodded.

My smile faded.

The next morning, from the playroom, where I was sequestered, I heard the doorbell ring. I looked over at Agnes, the young maid assigned the task of keeping an eye on me while Mr. McCormick visited. She was curled up on the window seat, thoroughly engrossed in the fashion section of *Godey's Lady's Book*.

The doorbell rang again.

I was desperately curious. Who was this man who could dent my father's iron demeanor? I had to get a glimpse!

Easing myself away from my toy soldiers, I tiptoed out of the playroom and down the long hallway. At the top of the stairs, I ducked and peeked between the railings.

Mr. McCormick stood in the foyer, a portly man of regal bearing, with graying hair and an even grayer goatee. He wore an impressive top hat, an elegant waist-coat and . . .

The world began to contract.

I could hear blood surging in my head, and my hands and feet began to tingle. It would happen soon. I knew it. The pondering. I tried to hold on, tried to turn back to the playroom. But my attention was already locked in. I made my way down the stairs and into the foyer, unable to pull my eyes or my mind away from Mr. McCormick's walking stick.

"Edgar!" I heard my father say sternly. His voice was so loud, I must have been standing right beside him. And yet I could not see him. In my mind, all was dark-ness, except for a shaft of light illuminating the object of my attention.

I stretched my hand toward it.

"The boy has fine taste," came another voice—Mr. McCormick's voice. "This walking stick once belonged to King Louis the Sixteenth himself. Here, boy, take a look."

My fingers locked around the mahogany stick. Oh, how silky the wood! How cool the golden handle against my cheek! Was that an eagle engraved in the gold? It was. And look at its green gemstone eyes! Green like the grass, like the spring leaves with the sun behind them, like the algae on the goldfish pond before the gardener skimmed it off . . .

They tell me I stood there for more than two hours,

clutching Mr. McCormick's cane; that Father grabbed my shoulders and through his clenched, white teeth hissed, "This is madness, Edgar. Stop at once!" But no matter what they did, they couldn't pry my fingers away or bring me back to reality. At one point, they say, I even bit Father's hand, drawing blood. I don't remember it. I don't remember any of it. Luncheon, of course, was ruined, and no business was discussed. Mr. McCormick finally went home without his stick, my father promising to return it as soon as possible.

"Why, Edgar?" Mother whimpered later that night. Her face was pale, her eyes wide. "Why did you do it? You've made your father furious."

Below, we could hear him storming about his study. Books flew. Feet pounded. Doors slammed.

As always after an episode, I was weak and lightheaded. Tears welled up in my eyes. I didn't want to be this way, but I couldn't help it. I didn't have any control over the ponderings. "I'm sorry," I managed to say. "I'm sorry."

She wrapped trembling arms around me. "As am I," she whispered.

The next morning before the sun had even risen, our driver, George, brought the carriage around to the servants' door, and I was stuffed inside like so much dirty laundry.

"What is happening?" I wailed. "Where's Mother?"

"Hush now, Master Edgar," Agnes said. She tossed my canvas bag of tin soldiers in after me. "You don't want to make a scene in front of the neighbors, now, do you?"

I clutched the bag to my chest and sniffled loudly.

"That's a good boy. Be brave." She slammed the carriage door, motioning for George to go.

But we had rolled only a few feet when the door was ripped open and Mother flung herself into the carriage. She pressed me to her chest, kissed my forehead over and over again.

"Oh, Edgar," she sobbed, and even in my confusion, I couldn't help noticing how disheveled she looked. She was still wearing last night's clothing, the wrinkled silk of her dress looking as tired as she did. Her face was tear-stained, and there was a darkening fist of a bruise forming on her left cheek. "He told me I couldn't say goodbye, but . . . oh, my darling!" With feverish hands she lifted my face toward her own, her voice pleading. "Try to forgive me, Edgar, try to understand. I'm not strong, not strong enough to stand up to him."

"Madam," cried Agnes, "please!" Grabbing my mother's arm, she pulled her away. Once again, the carriage door slammed.

"Edgar!" wailed Mother.

There came a snap of the whip, and we headed down the long driveway, gravel crackling under the wheels. I turned and looked back. Through my tears, I saw Mother hanging limp as a rag doll in Agnes's arms. And behind them, gazing out the dining room window, stood Father. Lifting a teacup with his bandaged hand, he took a sip. Then he drew the curtain.

The carriage rolled up Prairie Avenue past the stone-turreted mansions of Father's good friends Mr. Ogden and Mr. Potter before heading north along bustling Michigan Avenue. To my right stretched the lake, an endless blue as far as my eye could see. To my left, grain houses dominated the skyline: huge slate-surfaced storage sheds, rising higher than the steeples of the city's churches. We turned along the river, headed toward the tangle of rail lines. How was I to know that this would be the last time I would see any of this?

George pulled up before the train station and, taking my small hand firmly in his, dragged me through the mammoth steel shed. Steam engines sputtered. Bells clanged. Brakemen shouted, "Shee-caw-go! Shee-caw-go!"

I gripped my bag of tin soldiers even more tightly. "Where are we going, George?" I shouted above the din.

"North, Master Edgar, to your father's hunting lodge in Wisconsin," he replied.

I hadn't known Father owned a hunting lodge. I looked at the hastily packed suitcase George held in his other hand. And I understood. The episode with Mr. McCormick had been the last straw. Father had banished me.

The door of a first-class passenger car was flung

open. George pushed me up and in, then passed my suitcase to a gray-uniformed porter.

"You are coming with me, aren't you?" I asked. Surely Father didn't mean to send me on the train without a chaperone.

But George shook his head. "I'm sorry, young sir, but you're going to have to make the rest of the journey all by yourself."

*All by myself.*

I could barely comprehend it as the porter stowed my luggage and settled me on one of the car's velvet-upholstered seats.

*All by myself.*

I pressed my nose to the beveled-glass window as the car filled with other passengers. Then, after what seemed like an interminable wait, there came a furious blast of whistles, and the train at last slid from the station.

Oh, how bleak was the scenery through which I passed—miles of soot-covered factories, chimneys belching black smoke into the sky, mountains of slag and coal. Then the train tore through the grimy smoke and burst into the vast loneliness of the prairie. Chicago—my home—became nothing more than a dark smear on the horizon.

Holding tight to my tin soldiers, I pressed my cheek to the plush cushions and wept.

The train traveled on, the prairie eventually giving

way to rows of corn and sagging barns. It rattled past wooded ravines and through endless small farm settlements, stopping occasionally to let off or take on passengers. Finally, just after sundown, it stopped at a tiny train station.

"Here we are, young sir," said the porter.

I glanced out the window. A man wearing overalls stood on the dusty platform. It was obvious he was waiting for me.

It took only a moment to help me down the stairs and hand over my luggage.

I looked around, but in the dark saw little more than the press of shadowy trees. I smelled pine needles and woodsmoke. In the distance, an owl hooted.

The train hissed and rumbled away.

And the farmer led me to his wagon. With a flick of the reins, we were off, following a narrow, rutted trail that led deep into the woods. Were there werewolves in these woods? Witches, as in the story of Hansel and Gretel? Then the house appeared and I sighed with relief. It was an ordinary place with, I soon would discover, two bedrooms upstairs, and a kitchen, parlor and dining room downstairs. There was even a small library.

Someone tall and dour, dressed in deep black, met me at the door. "Good evening, sir," she said, her piercing eyes never leaving mine. "I am your housekeeper, Mrs. Usher."

I cannot remember her exact words now, but I

know she explained the arrangements. She was there to cook and serve meals, do laundry and tidy the house. If I needed a new shirt, she would buy one. If I needed a doctor, she would fetch one. She was not there to entertain me or play with me. She was *not* my companion. When she finished, she waited for a reply.

"When will Mother be here?" I asked. "When is Father coming?"

I saw a little smile of scorn touch her lips, and I guessed at once that she had been told about my ponderings and considered me mad. Something in the expression of her face, so cool and politely impersonal, told me that she would also be watching me, her eyes always upon me, reporting back to Father.

"Your parents are not coming," she said firmly. "No one is coming."

And as days turned to weeks, and weeks became months, I resigned myself to the truth of her words. No one *was* coming. Not Mother. Not Father. Not ever.

Thus I gave in more and more to my ponderings. And though I knew Mrs. Usher's eye was upon me, I easily dismissed her from my thoughts as I mused for long hours on the texture of a pinecone; became absorbed for the better part of a summer's day on a blue shadow slanting across the floor; lost myself for an entire winter's night in watching the steady flame of the gaslight. So many objects seized my attention, held me in thrall, that—how to explain this?—the years simply slipped by unnoticed. Summer became winter. Winter became summer again. And still I pondered. The winking brass of the bureau drawer knobs. A hairline crack in a glass paperweight.

And then . . . *the wallpaper.*

Pondering the wallpaper was unlike anything I had experienced before. Its whispers were clearer. More alive. And as I pondered the wallpaper, its patterns seemed to crawl deep inside me, revealing dark secrets . . . No! Reflecting my own darkness to me.

I could barely—just barely—make out a figure, skulking behind the confusing, uncertain curves of the wallpaper's pattern. It crouched and crept, provoking me with its sly coyness. But I was cleverer. I pressed my ear to the wallpaper. Yes . . . there! The faint thump of a heart. I held a candle close. Aha! I caught the figure out of the corner of my eye. It scuttled into the shadows.

And then I discerned something else. The wallpaper, which looked so solid and substantial by daylight, dissolved in the candle's glow. The roiling pattern shifted, taking on the shape of prison bars. The teeth above the bedstead clacked a warning. The glowering eyes blazed.

The skulking figure grew clearer, and I could see that it was a boy. A boy exactly like me, trapped within the malicious pattern. Alone.

*All by himself.*

The glowering eyes of the wallpaper watched the boy's every movement, while its teeth—those strong white teeth—kept guard, refusing to let the boy out.

I knew I had to help him. I had to free him!

With a howl of fury, I lunged at the paper. I pounded it with my fists, clawed at it with my fingernails until they were split and bloody. But still the paper clung stubbornly to the walls, thwarting me, enraging me.

"Hurry," urged the boy in the wallpaper.

I redoubled my efforts, snatching a letter opener from a bedside table and gouging at the paper. I stabbed it, raked at it, skinned it from the plaster wall as one would a pelt from a rabbit. And at long last the paper surrendered, peeling away in great sticky strips. Those glowering eyes grew wide with fright. The teeth clenched in terror. The boy, at last, was free! I laughed victoriously as scraps of the odious red-flocked stuff dripped to the floor like dried blood. I fell back, panting and drenched in sweat.

*Am I awake, or am I still pondering?*

With a moan, I buried my face in my trembling hands.


Bits of sticky paper still clung to my shaggy hair, and red flocking still dusted my white shirt when Father suddenly appeared in the library like an apparition.

"Are you real?" I asked. "Or are you a figment?"

Father did not answer. He was assessing me, sizing me up in that way of his, taking in my gray pallor, my overlong hair, my red-rimmed eyes. It had been only this morning that I'd awakened from my struggle with the wallpaper—three whole days of focus—and I was spent. But I knew that did not begin to explain the differences Father must have seen in me. Six years was a long time. I had changed from a boy to a man.

Asked Father, "Do you still suffer from those"—he searched for the word—"inclinations?"

I nodded.

He paused, collected himself, pulled his waistcoat straight. "No matter," he said. "I didn't make the trip to discuss that. Your mother is dead. She succumbed last week to cholera." He waited for my response.

I gave him none.

"Her last wish was that I come and see you myself."

As he talked I watched his thin pink lips parting to expose his hard teeth, gleaming white against his dark beard. Those teeth. How I wish to God I had never seen them!

"Have you nothing to say?" said Father.

I could not speak. The blood was boiling in my head, and my hands and feet were beginning to tingle.

From a distance I heard him say, "I shall have Mrs. Usher show me to my room." I heard the library door close behind him.

Then all became dark, but I could still see him—Father's face . . . his beard . . . his glowering eyes . . . those teeth. Those hard white teeth. Not a speck on their surface. Not a mark or indentation on their enamel. Perfect and glistening; now making a clacking sound, now a grinding sound.

*NO!*

I wrestled with my pondering, struggled against its strange and irresistible focus. But it was no use. Everything else faded away, and I was left with one mesmerizing thought—Father's teeth. They, and they alone, were all I could see. My mind's eye traveled over their surface, taking in their shape, their sharpness. They felt so real, as if I was holding them in my hand rather than my mind. My muscles tensed. My blood rose.

Night closed in on me, and still I pondered Father's teeth.

The morning mists came and went, and still I pondered.

A second night passed, and a day, and still I remained motionless as visions of Father's teeth floated above me—clenched, grimacing, commanding all my attention.

At last the clock in the hall chimed midnight and the spell was broken. I blinked, panting, suddenly free. In place of the spell, a feeling of dread began to creep over me. I had done something . . .

I searched my memory. But all that came to me was a dim recollection of a man's voice crying out.

"What was it?" I asked myself.

My question was answered by a pounding on the library door. It banged open and two gray-uniformed policemen filled the doorway. Behind them stood Mrs. Usher. "There he is!" she shouted, pointing at me. "There's the madman."

I shook my head in confusion.

The first policeman pointed at my shirt.

I looked down. The white cotton was soaked with blood.

The second policeman grabbed my arm.

It was covered with scratches, and the crescent-moon imprints of human fingernails.

And then I remembered.

Oh, God, I remembered!

My eyes fell on the wooden cigar box sitting on the desk. I had put it there when . . . Shaking off the policeman's hand, I bounded over to it.

"He's going for a revolver!" shrieked Mrs. Usher.

"Stop or I'll shoot!" shouted one of the policemen.

I ignored his warning and snatched up the box.

"I'm warning you, drop it!"

There came the soft click of a gun's hammer being drawn back. But I was too feverish and agitated to care. I wrestled open the box. It slipped from my trembling fingers and fell with a crash to the floor. Oh, God . . . no!

Mrs. Usher screamed.

The policeman fired.

I felt a white-hot bolt of pain as I, too, fell to the floor.

The last things I saw, spilling from that wooden box, were a pair of bloody pliers and Father's thirty-two hard white teeth.

"Jeez," croaked Mike. He fell back against Carol Anne's gravestone, gripping the cold granite for support as the strength seeped out of his body, just drained out like water from a leaky bucket. "No wonder the guy looks so . . . so . . . hollowed out."

"Yeah, that was awful, all right," said a new voice, a female voice.

*Truly* awful. Mike shuddered as Edgar retreated to the shadowy branches of the willow tree. "How could something like that happen?" Mike wondered out loud. "How could a father be so cruel?"

"Good old parents," the girl said, raising her right eyebrow sarcastically. "They bring you into the world just to drive you crazy or dump you, you know?"

Mike turned to look at her now—a wiry girl with attitude. "You have a story you want to tell?"

She gave him a withering look. "Like why else would I have waited around all friggin' night?" Stepping into the rapidly waning circle of moonlight, she hollered, "Okay, you freaks, listen up."

# TRACY

## 1959–1974

YOU WANT TO KNOW why I was standing on the sow's front porch that night? Because I didn't have any other choice, that's why. See, it was either the sow's house or child protective custody, and frankly, I'd rather have my guts pulled out through my nose than spend another night in the ESC—that's the Emergency Services Center, for those of you with nice, comfy homes.

The sow pushed open the screen door with her dough-fat hand, and a smell like dirty scalp escaped from the house. I wasn't surprised. I mean, let's face it, there was a sagging blue chest of drawers leaning against the porch railing and an open bag of cat food spilling down the stairs. Chicken-and-liver pellets had gone *crunch-crunch-crunch* beneath my platform shoes as I'd kicked aside papers and books and bits and pieces of busted-up sewing machine on my way to her door. I'd even counted, like, seven pairs of identical white tennis shoes piled in a corner. Crazy!

The social worker standing next to me tried to peer past the sow's fleshy bulk into the house. I could tell he was unsure about leaving me here, didn't like the look of the place. He asked, "Do you mind if I step in, ma'am? Take a look around?"

"I certainly *do* mind," she said. She straightened her beefy shoulders, tried to push out her sagging-to-the-waist boobs. "It's bad enough being saddled with the girl for the weekend. I won't have you in my house, too."

The two locked eyes, and for a second I thought they might go at each other, you know?

Then the sow said, "Either sign her over right here or take her back where she came from."

The social worker backed down. The last thing he wanted was to return me to his car, drive me all the way down to the ESC, especially after I'd called him "donkey breath" and smeared a booger under the car's headrest. So he nodded, pulled out some paperwork, got the sow to sign on the dotted line. "Good luck, Tracy," he said, acting all sincere the way grown-ups do when they can't wait to be somewhere else. Then he practically danced down the littered walk to his car.

Mission accomplished: kid dumped.

The sow locked eyes with me now. "You're Tracy," she said.

*Duh!* "Yeah," I went.

"I'm your aunt Viola," she said. "I guess you'll have to come in." She pushed open the screen door a few more inches, just enough for me and my overnight bag to slip in sideways.

"Whoa!" I went. "No way!"

Her house was packed to the gills. Actually, packed to the gills doesn't begin to describe it. Imagine the entire contents of a town dump squeezed into a five-room bungalow on Chicago's North Side. Now do you catch my drift? The whole place was a mess of empty pizza boxes, rumpled magazines, sun-faded lawn chairs, stained clothes, tattered stuffed animals, buckets and boxes of screws and strings, towers of newspapers, wind chimes, dented lamp shades, busted umbrellas. You name it, she'd saved it. Piled floor-to-ceiling. More, more, more. Room after room after room.

"No way!" I said again.

Aunt Viola ignored me. "I suppose I have to feed you something," she said all martyr-like. "I have hot dogs." She paused. "And sherbet. I have some orange sherbet."

"Whatever." I was too busy looking around to think about food.

"I'll have more variety day after tomorrow. That's when the delivery boy leaves my groceries on the front step," she said. "I don't go out, and I don't let people in, so hot dogs'll have to do until then."

As she waddled down a narrow canyon that'd been cleared through the mountains of debris, her mammoth hips bumped into a wooden sled propped precariously against a rusted bedspring. The sled fell, knocking into a tower of twine-tied shoe boxes, which brought down an avalanche of soda cans, board games, paperback books and a bowling ball.

"This house is a friggin' booby trap!" I shouted, covering my head and plowing through the junk.

Aunt Viola didn't even flinch.

"Why don't you throw some of this junk out?"

She snorted. "You young people nowadays think everything's disposable."

I noticed a laundry basket full of, like, a hundred used margarine tubs. "Some things *are* disposable."

Aunt Viola just kept waddling.

I followed along behind her, being real careful not to bump into anything. The deeper we went into the house, the stronger that dirty scalp stink got. It reminded me of something dark, something I couldn't quite put my finger on.

We reached the kitchen. Every surface was piled high, and every one of the cabinet doors hung open, their insides a ceramic jigsaw puzzle of mugs and bowls and plates and platters. And all of a sudden I got this itch to play Ker Plunk. You know that game? It's the one where you try to pull out a stick without letting all the marbles tumble. Except in this case, I wanted to see if I could slip out a saucer without causing a clattering tidal wave of china.

Aunt Viola took a cleared pathway to the refrigerator, and I winced even before I saw inside. If the sink and countertops looked like this, I could only imagine what science experiments were growing in there—loaves of once-white bread fuzzy with blue mold; black slime floating on the surface of an open can of fruit cocktail.

But the fridge's insides were surprisingly white and empty, the cleanest place in the house, probably because food was the only thing that didn't get saved around here. I mean, it was pretty obvious Aunt Viola enjoyed her groceries.

She took a pack of hot dogs out of the meat tray and sidled down the path toward the stove. Only one of the burners was clear of debris. The rest of the stovetop was buried and the oven door hung open, stuffed too full of baking pans and casserole dishes to ever be closed. Or used. Her thick fingers dropped two hot dogs into a saucepan of water. She turned the stove's dial.

I took a closer look at her. She was padded everywhere—belly, back, shoulders, thighs. Even her ankles and elbows were soft. Blubber bulged behind her knees. Blubber had filled out the wrinkles and sags in her face, too, leaving her looking like some weird over-sized porcelain doll complete with grayish-blond finger curls and these crazy eyebrows she'd penciled in above her cold blue eyes.

She can't be in *my* family, can she? "How are we related, again?" I asked.

The water boiled. "I'm your great-aunt. Your mother's mother's sister."

I tried to work this out in my head as she forked two steaming hot dogs onto a paper plate and handed me a half-empty mustard bottle.

What, no bun?

She sat me at the only cleared space at the table. It was sticky and sprinkled with what looked like cracker crumbs, although in this place, one could never tell. I took a closer look, made sure it wasn't maggots. Then I squirted a splotch of mustard onto my plate, picked up a hot dog carefully so I didn't burn my fingers and dipped it into the mustard like it was a French fry or something. *Bon appétit,* right?

"So," she said, crossing her big arms across her bigger belly, "let's get acquainted, shall we?"

I started on the second dog. "What do you want to know?" You nosy, hoarding cow.

She leaned down until her china-doll face was just inches from mine. "It's what I want *you* to know," she said. Her voice sounded like a wasp in a glass jar—angry and trapped. "I'm doing this—letting you stay here—against my better judgment. I don't like people in my house. I don't trust people in my house."

I arched my right eyebrow, a sarcastic gesture I'd been practicing forever. "So why'd you say yes? I mean, it's not like we're some lovey-dovey family or anything like that. Heck, I never even knew I had a great-aunt until yesterday."

She arched her right eyebrow even more sarcastically

than me. "I thought I'd get in trouble with the authorities if I said no. The last thing I want is any trouble with the authorities."

"What, you murder somebody or something?"

"Sherbet?" She waddled up the path to the refrigerator, pulled out a pint carton and worked her way back to the table. Somewhere along the way she'd picked up a spoon, maybe from one of the half dozen drawers that were hanging out like dogs' tongues. She peeled the sticky lid off the pint, then dropped the sherbet and the spoon in front of me.

First no buns, and now no bowl. Yeah, this place was first-class.

"So what's your mother in jail for this time?" she asked. "Stealing some guy's wallet? Public brawling?"

I paused, pretending to be on the emotional edge. "I don't want to talk about it. I'm too . . . overwrought." I stroked that last word, giving it just the right amount of angst. I even quivered my lower lip a little like I was about to burst into tears, you know? It was a great performance—got the social workers every time.

But it didn't work on fat Aunt Viola. "You're here just until your mother makes bail. And during that time, you're going to do exactly as I say."

She was starting to freak me out, not like the "there's a zombie around the corner" kind of freak-out, but the "you better not mess with me" kind of freak-out. So I said, "I've got a razor blade taped to my thigh." It was a lie. I was unarmed. But it sounded good. Authentic, you know, like I was a real delinquent. I made myself look right into those cold blue eyes of hers, met her gaze, bluffing.

Aunt Viola didn't even blink. "Done with that?" She pointed to the melting pint of sherbet in front of me. Without knowing it, I'd stabbed the spoon into its softening orange innards over and over again. I pushed it away.

We left the sherbet melting on the table—why was I not surprised?—and I followed her around the house. We took the cleared trails. There was no other way unless you were a mountain goat, and it dawned on me that each trail led someplace necessary—bed, fridge, john. The whole place reeked of that dirty scalp smell, and everything was covered with a gritty white film, like the house had a bad case of dry skin. It was pretty obvious the place was falling apart. The floors slanted, and there were lightning-bolt cracks all over the ceiling. It was like the house was collapsing in on itself, buckling under the weight of all that stuff.

For a second I changed my mind about staying there. Then I thought of the ESC, with its rows of torture cots, and its pathetic little kids crying all night for their mommies because they hadn't figured out the score yet, and those oh-so-sincere social workers who were constantly in my face, trying to quote, "break through your emotional walls," unquote. And you know what? Aunt Viola's didn't seem so bad after all.

But it would have been even better if I'd had a razor blade, you know?

We came to a fork in the trail.

"I sleep in there," Aunt Viola said. She pointed to the right, where the trail cut through a wall of cardboard boxes and into a bedroom. Through the growing darkness, I could see a double bed, its sheets a tangled knot, half of it hiding under a jumble of cookie boxes and catalogs.

"What about me?" I asked.

She pointed to the left. "There's a sofa in the living room," she said. "In the corner there. You'll need to clear it off."

"What's that?" I asked. There was a door in the hallway, strangely clear of debris. It had a heavy, industrial-strength padlock on it.

"That's off-limits," she said. "The stairs to the attic."

"Why off-limits?"

"You ask too many questions."

I reached out and tested the lock just to rattle her chain. "Ooh, nice and tight," I said. "So what do you keep up there? The family jewels?" Or just more broken typewriters and rusty sinks?

She grabbed my arm, her fat hand squeezing with an anaconda grip. "Listen, girly." Yeah, she actually said "girly." "You just mind your own business. Understand?"

I shook her off. "Jeez, I was only teasing. Can't you take a joke?"

"I never joke," she said, and her eyes looked dead and flat. "Never."

"Oh," I went. The minute I said it, I wanted to kick myself. Like, really, what kind of snappy comeback was "Oh"?

"Off-limits," Aunt Viola hissed again.

"All right, already," I said.

Aunt Viola stood there glowering, her hands on her elephant hips, and watched as I squeezed into the living room and over to a sofa that was buried beneath two feet of books, papers and magazines. I looked around. No sheets or pillows, just an ancient lap robe that looked like it had been crocheted by Martha Washington. I pushed everything into a heap on the floor, then sat cross-legged on the gritty cushions.

"Comfortable?" Aunt Viola called out.

Was she joking?

"Cozy as a coffin," I called back.

I heard the floorboards creak under her weight as she headed toward her bed, and then I was alone. I sighed. It couldn't have been later than ten p.m. Too early for bed. Besides, I was still feeling a little ambushed by the day. This place. Her. I knew I couldn't possibly fall asleep yet. Halfheartedly, I looked around for a television, but knew I wouldn't find one. Bummer. I could have used a little *Chico and the Man* distraction right about then.

Bored, I pushed around the heap of books and papers with my foot. A liver-spotted copy of *Life* magazine surfaced, a picture of Frank Sinatra on its cover. There was an empty album sleeve from some band called the Tijuana Brass, a tattered composition book, a bent post-card of the John Hancock Building, and . . .

*What's this?*

I reached down and snagged a scrapbook—water-stained, its edges curling—out of the mess. A ghostly puff of dust rose as I opened it. It was all newspaper clippings. Page after page of yellowing old newspaper clippings. All of them were from the 1920s. And they were all about Aunt Viola.

I read the scrapbook from beginning to end. Every clipping on every page. And pretty soon, all those bits and pieces came together to form a story—the Story of Aunt Viola. And man, was it a crazy one.

She was born Viola O'Hara, and she began her life of crime as a petty thief in a bad neighborhood on the near North Side called Little Hell. By the time she was in her twenties, she was a small-time racketeer who paid for her fancy dresses (made to accommodate the three guns she usually carried) and her florist business (a cover for what she *really* did) by running booze from Canada. Twice the Genna family, believing she was muscling in on their territory, tried to gun her down—the first time in front of a thousand people on opening night after a show outside the LaSalle Theatre; the second time while dancing the Charleston at the Aragon Ballroom. But Viola was a bet-ter shot. She made headlines. Her picture was in every paper. Reporters dubbed her the doll-faced moll. The Genna family dubbed her a menace. And Al Capone—the most famous gangster of all—called her sweetheart. That is, of course, until the day he tried slapping her around her apartment. That was when Viola pulled a four-inch knife from her garter belt and turned Al into Scarface. Needless to say, he never called her sweetheart again.

According to a long article in the *Chicago Tribune*, Viola did fall in love with this guy named Pete Winters, a war hero who worked in her florist shop. Pete was on the up-and-up, as straight an arrow as they came. Viola had never known such a hardworking, decent guy. He somehow managed to touch the few tender chords inside her. She decided to give up her life of crime, move away to Colorado with Pete, become a respectable married dame. But she needed money. So she swallowed her pride, cinched up her courage and went to the richest man she knew—Al Capone. I guess she was willing to risk it all for love, you know?

So what happened next? I got the rest of the gory details straight from this old-time pulp-fact magazine called *True Crime*. The facts seemed to me like they might have been a little dicey, but the story was a juicy one. According to *True Crime*, this is how things went down:

"What do you say we let bygones be bygones?" Viola says to Capone. "I'm here to do you a favor and sell you my portion of the Canadian whiskey business."

"How much?" asks Capone through gritted teeth.

175

"I'm a reasonable woman," replies Viola. "And we've known each other a long time."

Capone smiles a tight little smile.

"How does fifty thousand dollars sound?" asks Viola. "Fair?"

"Done," says Al. He writes Viola an IOU. Tells her it's good to see her again. Kisses her cheek goodbye. Maybe he even touches the scar on his face.

The following evening just before closing, the phone in the florist shop rings.

Pete Winters answers.

"I'd like to place an order for a funeral tomorrow," says the man on the other end, who claims his name is Mr. Brown. "Am I too late?"

"Not at all, not at all," says Pete.

"Okay," says Mr. Brown. "I want a wreath of red roses. A real big one. Say five hundred dollars' worth?"

"Fine," says Pete. "We can do that."

"I'll come in and pick it up tomorrow, around noon," says Mr. Brown.

"We can deliver it if you want," says Pete.

"No, this is something I want to do for myself," says Mr. Brown.

"Of course," says Pete. "Glad to oblige." He thanks Mr. Brown for his business, checks the cooler to make sure there are enough roses to fill the order, then goes out to dinner with Viola.

At noon the next day, Pete and another employee

named Jim Holloway are bent over the worktable in the florist shop, wiring the last of the roses together, when a blue touring car rolls up to the curb. Three men climb out; the driver stays where he is, motor running. A boy playing on the sidewalk notices that the man in the middle has a scar on his face. "Get lost, kid," says the man. The kid scampers away. The men push open the florist's door. The bell jangles. Holloway looks up. Uh-oh, he thinks. I recognize *that* face. He ducks into the back room.

"Hello, gentlemen," says Pete. "Here for the flowers?" He steps forward, shears in one hand, the other held out for a handshake.

The man with the scar takes it. "I'm Mr. Brown," he says.

Pete smiles and nods.

Holloway makes it to the back room and shuts the door.

A few minutes go by. From his hiding place in back, Holloway hears chitchat. A couple of laughs. Then—*bang!*

The first shot goes wild. But not the next ones. They're fired at such close range that they leave powder burns on Pete's wool suit. The last shot is a head shot—the coup de grâce, is what the Mob likes to call it. Holloway waits until the men are gone before creeping back out. Pete is on his back in a puddle of blood and rose petals. He never knows he's been arranging flowers for his own funeral.

The *True Crime* story ended there. Eager to know more, I turned the page of the scrapbook and found a batch of clippings from some old newspaper called the *Chicago Daily News*. I read slowly, piecing together the rest of Aunt Viola's story.

She obviously spared no expense when it came to Pete's funeral. His silver and gold coffin cost ten thousand dollars; its makers had it sent from Philadelphia by express train in a private baggage car. Musicians from the Chicago Symphony Orchestra played "Ave Maria," and the city's cardinal delivered the eulogy.

There was a picture of Viola on the front page. She was, like, two hundred pounds skinnier, wearing black satin and a full-length mink coat. From behind her black veil, a reporter overheard her say, "It's time to get back into the florist business."

In no time flat, Viola had gunned down the leaders of two rival South Side gangs and seized control of their bootleg operations. She tracked down Mr. Brown's accomplices and allegedly killed them by shoving a rose stem into their brains through their left nostrils while they begged for mercy. Then, with her Thompson submachine gun blazing, she shot up the Lexington Hotel, Capone's headquarters down on Michigan and Cermak. Capone escaped through one of his secret tunnels. But that didn't stop Viola from taking a sledgehammer to his Tiffany lamps, his gold-plated bathroom fixtures, his beloved lavender-tiled tub. She stormed his basement vault, too, emptying it of more than a million dollars in gold coins. Then she just disappeared. Most people figured Capone caught up with her, gave her a pair of cement shoes and tossed her into the Chicago River. But a few speculated she had gotten away.

The last article in Aunt Viola's scrapbook was still white-paper new, printed just a little over a year ago on the forty-fifth anniversary of the Lexington shoot-out. "Where is the Doll-Faced Moll now?" the article asked.

"Right here," I muttered to myself. "She's right here."

Was I scared?

Sort of.

But I was even more curious. What if Aunt Viola really *did* get away with Al Capone's gold? What did she do with it all? I looked around the grody, overstuffed living room. She sure as heck hadn't spent it here, right? Like, this wasn't exactly Millionaires' Row. So where was it?

I remembered reading once about this loony old lady who stashed hundreds of thousands of dollars' worth of loot in crazy places all over her house. Like, she froze her emerald rings into ice trays and hid her diamond necklace in a cracker box. Maybe Aunt Viola had done something like that, too. I mean, she was nuts enough. But where would she have hidden it? I sat there on the sofa with the scrapbook, wondering.

I must have fallen asleep, because I woke with a start.

Someone was trying to tiptoe down the pathway without making a sound—a pretty impossible task if that someone was the size of a baby hippo. Floorboards groaned. Mountains of stuff rattled and shook. I heard the telltale creak of a door, then the heaving, straining, panting sounds of Aunt Viola climbing a flight of stairs. Her heavy footfalls caused the whole house to shudder and shed trickles of plaster.

Off-limits, huh?

I got up and waded through the books and papers until I found the pathway that led from the living room to the hall. The door to the attic was open a crack. A key on a red satin ribbon, like the kind florists tie around bouquets of roses, still dangled from the now-sprung lock. I touched it, causing the ribbon to sway back and forth.

What was up there?

And as soon as I asked the question, I *knew*. I *knew* what was up there. It was obvious, wasn't it? It was Al Capone's gold. Aunt Viola had stashed it in the attic. I bet she was up there counting the coins that very minute.

I thought about charging up the stairs, bursting in on her, shouting, "Caught ya, you fat, lying mobster!"

But a better idea was already wiggling its way into my brain. Why not help myself to a little of that loot? I wouldn't take much, just enough to say so long forever to Aunt Viola and her weird, stinking house; and to my useless mother and her long police record; and to the ESC, which could never, ever be a real home.

I grinned. Oh, yeah, by tomorrow morning I'd be hitching west on Interstate 80, free and easy, my pockets bulging with Scarface's gold.

I went back to the sofa, pulled the ancient lap robe up to my chin, traced the cracks in the ceiling and waited.

Time crept by.

Finally, Aunt Viola dragged herself down the stairs. The house shook, and I couldn't help wondering if the steps would hold. But they did. Minutes later I heard her mattress springs groan. Minutes after that, I heard her snore.

It was my turn now.

It was easy to sneak into her bedroom. Easier still to swipe the key off her nightstand. Aunt Viola snored louder than a Harley without a muffler, drowning out any giveaway noises, like the crunch of plaster beneath my shoes and the *ting* sound the key on its ribbon made when it accidentally bumped into a half-empty bottle of soda.

I had the attic door unlocked and open in less time than it took to say "mobster." Behind it was a flight of narrow, sagging stairs. There was no light switch, but a window at the very top let in a shaft of moonlight. I began to climb, quietly, quietly. The attic stank of dirty scalp. It wasn't until I reached the top landing that I realized the stairs were clutter free. For the first time since I'd arrived at Aunt Viola's house, I hadn't had to wind, wade or pick my way through junk.

I came to another door. It was partway open, revealing nothing but darkness.

Why was I hesitating? Because all of a sudden, I felt a little scared—those narrow stairs, the moonlight, an *attic*. Suddenly, I remembered all the late-night horror movies I'd watched where some dimwitted girl walks into a slimy cellar or cobwebby attic and the whole time I'm yelling at the TV screen, going, "What are you, stupid or something?"

But that was the movies, and this was real life. There weren't any zombies or chain-saw-wielding serial killers hiding behind that door. What there was—I knew it— was gold.

I gave the door a push and it swung open, the moonlight piercing the blackness. And it was hard to tell, but I thought . . . yes, there in front of me was . . . a bunch of *dummies.* You know, like store mannequins, and they were arranged around a long table. Six dummies, actually, three on one side, three on the other. They were sitting in chairs and dressed in old-time clothes—fedora hats and overcoats—all neat and tidy as well-loved dolls. As a matter of fact, everything about this room was neat and tidy. There was no junk. No clutter. No dust or plaster grit.

And no safe or pile of gold, either.

I crept into the room for a closer look, and the stench hit me so hard I thought I was going to puke. It was totally gross, like if you scrape the surface of your tongue in the morning and then smell it. You know, sort of moist and decayed. Breathing through my mouth, I looked around.

There was a bottle of whiskey and six shot glasses in the middle of the table, and in front of each of the dummies sat a crazy object, like a violin case or a box of cigars. There were name plates, too, and I bent down for a closer look. BUGS MORAN, read one name plate. JOHN DILLINGER, read another. The dummy closest to me was labeled AL CAPONE.

Now we were getting somewhere. "Where's the loot, buster?" I said, goofing around. Even with my nostrils pinched shut, it was a pretty good mobster imitation. I looked directly into the dummy's face.

Except it wasn't a dummy face. It was a . . . a *real* face. Withered. Dried. Horrible. Its leathery lips were drawn back over yellowing teeth in an eternal sneer. There was a gaping black hole where the nose should have been, and the eyes, wrinkled like raisins, were sunken in the eye sockets. In the green-tinged skin stretched tight across the cheekbones, I could just make out the shadow of a scar. And now—*now!*—I knew what that smell was, that smell that stank up every crevice of the groaning, sagging house. It wasn't dirty scalp or tongue scrapings. It was death. The smell of rotting human head.

I looked around the table. Correction: *six* rotting heads!

Six rotting heads mounted on six mannequin bodies!

I fell back, and a weird sound came out of my throat, not a scream but a croak. I wheeled, ready to run.

Her bulk filling the entire door, there stood Aunt Viola, blocking the way.

She looked sullen, her lower lip pushed out as if her feelings were hurt. "You have no right. You shouldn't be here."

"I agree," I said. "I shouldn't be here." I took a step toward the door.

But Aunt Viola just waddled into the room, the floor-boards complaining. She took a kerosene lamp from a nearby shelf, lit it, then shut the door behind her.

"It was easy for me," she said, and her voice sounded faraway, you know? "I was a florist. I had a paneled truck. When I drove through the cemetery gates, nobody—not the groundskeepers or the gravediggers—ever questioned why I was there. So easy. I dug them up and simply plucked off their heads."

"Heads?" I repeated stupidly.

"It's just like flowers," she went on. "You don't take the whole plant, you just take the blossom." She brought her sausage-sized thumb and index finger together when she said this, as if delicately pinching off a bloom.

"Now I run the whole show. I'm the boss. I tell the boys what to do, and they obey." She stroked the back of Bugs Moran's head, opened the box of cigars and stuck one between Capone's yellow teeth. "I take good care of my boys. I make sure they have everything they want."

"That's . . . that's sick!" It was out of my mouth before I could stop it.

She turned those cold blue eyes on me, and I could actually see them harden. They glinted like two marbles that had been pressed into her doughy face. "That's what everyone seems to think," she said, and that angry wasp voice was back. "And that's why I can't let you leave here . . . ever."

Moving quicker than I'd ever thought possible, Aunt Viola lunged. She wrapped her huge hands around my neck and began to squeeze.

I clawed at her face, but that just made her grip tighten.

"I told you to stay out of the attic," she hissed in my ear. "I told you."

She squeezed tighter with each word, until the room spun. I clawed at my own neck, at her fingers—so strong for such an old woman. My hands slapped the wooden table, grasping for anything. I felt a sleeve and I pulled. I pulled hard.

John Dillinger seemed to leap out of his chair, and out of the corner of my eye I saw his head go straight up in the air, then drop and roll across the table, knocking over the shot glasses before bouncing over the edge. It hit the wooden floor with the exact sound a jack-o'-lantern makes when it's smashed on the sidewalk.

"Nooooo!" wailed Aunt Viola. She dropped me like a used tissue.

I lay there, stunned, for a heartbeat. But I wasn't going to die in this attic. No way.

Aunt Viola was trying to get down on her hands and knees, not an easy thing for her. Dillinger's head had rolled under the table, just out of reach, and she swiped at it with a fat, clumsy paw.

Pulling myself to my feet, I staggered out the door and tripped down the stairs, my legs all wobbly and jellylike.

Behind me I heard Aunt Viola bellowing. She pounded after me. The very timbers of the house shook.

I stumbled down the pathway, knocking over boxes, bouncing and bumping into bicycles and rusty sinks. I couldn't walk straight. I couldn't think straight. It was like I was drunk, you know? Like Aunt Viola had squeezed out all my juice. The house, with its crazy canyons and winding trails, had become a maze. I went in circles. I kept coming to dead ends. Finally, I got to a door.

"Don't open that!" shouted Aunt Viola. She was in the middle of the staircase, her eyes blazing at me.

"Watch me!" I cried.

And two things happened at once. The stairs groaned and split open, and the rotted wood swallowed Aunt Viola, the railings and the plaster walls folding in on top of her. She screamed, a long, piercing wail followed by silence. And then the whole house started to shiver and quake. Piles of newspapers fell. Towers of garbage tipped. Things were crashing, smashing all around me.

I pulled open the door, what I thought was the way out. But it wasn't the way out, it was a closet, and before I could close it more junk came crashing down, knocking me over, covering me. I struggled to stand, but the whole house was moving, shifting, leaning. I fell flat on the floor, gasping as junk hurtled on top of me. There was an ear-shattering crack as the ceiling gave way, and suddenly the attic was on top of me, too. I couldn't move. I couldn't breathe.

I smelled gas. Then smoke. And I knew the furnace, or the stove, or that crazy kerosene lamp, had caught fire, and I struggled, but the weight of fifty years' junk pressed me down. My lungs were squeezed empty, and as the world faded, I managed to turn my head. Through the dust and smoke, I saw a man, just inches away. He was dressed in a pinstripe suit, a thick cigar clenched in his lifeless gray mouth, a scar on his left cheek. And all around him, like gold dust, was a sprinkling of coins.

The night sky was lightening to gray as Tracy ended her story.

"Scarface's gold!" Johnnie whistled appreciatively. "I'da traded my last pair of knickers to see that."

Lily shuddered. "Not if it meant meeting scary Aunt Viola."

"She *was* a monster," agreed David. "And if anyone knows about monsters, it's me."

"You know what I think?" Scott said. "I think we've *all* confronted monsters in some way or other—monsters, evil, the dark and unexplained."

"Father," muttered Edgar.

"Yeah, don't forget to add dear old Dad to the list of creepy-crawlies," said Tracy.

The others nodded.

"*Resolute,*" Scott said, still following his chain of thought. "That's the word. However things got twisted, whatever weird stuff was thrown at us, we faced up to it. Sure, we died, but we dealt with that, you know? We even learned from it. And that's something. Maybe it's *more* than something."

The ghosts nodded, moving closer. Standing around Mike in a broken circle, they fell silent, suddenly solemn.

It was Gina who broke the stillness. "I think that's it," she said. "We're all done. Everyone's told their story."

"Good thing," observed Rich, "because it's almost morning."

Johnnie looked hard at Mike. "And you know what *that* means, don'tcha?"

Fear stirred in Mike's belly. "No," he said, his voice cracking. "I'm . . . I'm not sure what it means." He looked around at the ring of ghosts, his eyes moving from face to face, trying to read their expressions. And it came back to him then, what the voice in his head had whispered earlier, so many stories ago:

*It's a sign when the dead appear. A sign of your own death.*

Mike shook his head. "I don't want to die."

For a moment nothing moved. Even the wind stilled.

Then Evelyn giggled. Blanche joined in.

"Die?" repeated David, shaking his head.

"You got it all wrong, kid," said Johnnie. "We didn't bring you here to plant you six feet under."

"We wanted—no, we *needed*—to tell our stories," explained Rich. "And more importantly, we needed our stories to be *heard*."

Gesturing toward the others, David added, "Carol Anne . . . Gina . . . *all* of us brought you here to listen."

"Don't you see?" said Lily. "We all died without the chance to tell our stories. We may just be specters in this world, but our stories, if they are remembered and retold, become real and solid and alive."

"It's freaky weird, but totally true," said Tracy. "Once you hear a story, it becomes part of you. It can't die."

"And neither can we," said Blanche.

Gina nodded. "Now we can all move on."

Mike felt dizzy. Once again he was forced to grip the rough edge of Carol Anne's gravestone. In the growing light of dawn, he looked down at his hands. They looked so young and solid and *alive*. And he couldn't help it, couldn't put a lid on the stew of emotions—relief, sorrow, gratitude—that boiled up inside him. He swiped at his sudden tears, cleared his throat.

"Why me?" he finally managed to ask. "Why not somebody else?"

"Because you almost died last night," replied David.

"What?"

"The road," explained Rich. "Your hurrying. You couldn't have known that the bridge over Salt Creek was out."

"You would have come up on it too fast," said Gina. "You would have tried to put on your brakes, but—"

"*Splat!*" cried Tracy, a bit too enthusiastically.

Mike slumped against the gravestone.

"Don'tcha get it, dumb ox?" said Johnnie. "The only people who can see and hear us are those who are knocking at death's door."

"Those who have already drawn close to our world," added Scott.

Mike was beginning to understand. "Carol Anne saved me," he said, thinking aloud. "And . . . and brought me here to listen."

"That's right," said Lily. "Every year on the anniversary of her death she leads someone to the cemetery— someone our age, someone like you who can listen. This year it was *our* turn to tell our stories."

Mike looked around at the rows of tombstones. All those lives cut short, he thought. All those stories.

David broke into his thoughts. "The sun's almost up. Time for you to go home."

"And time for us to go, too," said Evelyn.

Later Mike would recall that it was like watching an old black-and-white film, the ghosts' images jumping and flickering, fading in and out. First substantial and then transparent. Solid, then ethereal. In the next second, they were drawn upward, lifted by a wind he could not feel. The cemetery itself seemed to exhale, a contented sigh that sounded almost human.

"See ya, schmuck," Johnnie called out.

"But not too soon," Gina hastily added.

What remained of their images flickered once more.

"Collin!" Lily squealed with joy.

And then they were gone.

Early-morning sunlight, soft and hazy, poked through the trees' bare branches, dappling the gravestones with specks of gold. Mike turned and saw the saddle shoes he had flung away the night before lying in a tangle of underbrush. Picking them up, he carefully placed them side by side at the foot of Carol Anne's grave.

"Take care," he whispered. "All of you."

Then, with the October sun warming his skin, he slipped back through the hole in the gate and down the dirt path to where his car was still parked on the side of the road.

He drove home . . . slowly.

# WHERE THE BONES LIE:
## A NOTE FROM THE AUTHOR

You can blame my fondness for ghost stories on my mother. She was forever telling tales of strange events that took place in our town. "Did you know that the Wynekoop mansion over on Sixth Street used to be called the House of Weird Death?" she would say, her voice growing hushed and mysterious. Or, "It's rumored that a ghost dog haunts Greenwood Cemetery." Then my sister Carole and I—huddled beneath a shared blanket, mashed together as close as we could get—would beg, "Tell us! Tell us!" And Mom would spin hair-raising tales about a corpse that wouldn't decay, or a phantom-filled trolley car, or a seaweed-covered ghost pilot whose plane went down in Lake Michigan during World War II.

Years later I realized that her stories, like most ghost stories, were inspired by memory and myth—by local legend and folklore, and by spooky tales told around the campfire. But above all, they were inspired by truth—by nearby places, real-life people, actual events. This connection with facts and history made her stories real . . . and real creepy! Fantasy suddenly became possibility. And as I listened, fear tickling my spine with its chilly fingers, I thought, *This* could happen to me. The idea was both thrilling and terrifying.

It was also enlightening. The best ghost stories, I learned, should always include a kernel of truth. And the stories in this book certainly do. Set in Chicago's very real neighborhoods and suburbs, they are shot through with the city's tragic, sometimes violent, but always intriguing history. Why Chicago? Because it is the spookiest place I know.

**Mike**—White Cemetery really does exist. Located off a sparsely populated country road near the suburb of Barrington, Illinois, the place is notorious for ghost sightings. Over the years, people have reported seeing floating orbs, and phantom cars, and even a "magic house" that appears and disappears as baffled witnesses look on. Creepy? You bet. The perfect setting for Mike's story.

**Gina**—While her story is fiction, many of its details—the depiction of an Italian American neighborhood in the early 1960s, the real terror of being trapped inside a blazing schoolroom—were drawn from firsthand accounts of the tragedy that struck Our Lady of the Angels School on the city's west side. On December 1, 1958, a fire tore through the Catholic grammar school, killing ninety-two students and three nuns and seriously injuring another hundred children. A former pupil later admitted to setting the blaze (as well as to starting other smaller fires throughout the neighborhood) but was never charged with the crime. Transcripts of actual interviews conducted by fire department investigators—as reported in David Cowan and John Kuenster's book *To Sleep with the Angels*—were especially helpful in fleshing out the character of a child arsonist. And a trip to Our Lady of the Angels (rebuilt in 1960 on the same site, and just a ten-minute drive from my house) helped me visualize my fictional school's layout.

**Johnnie**—I grew up hearing endless stories about Depression-era Chicago. My parents, who'd spent their childhoods there, often talked about the city's fifty percent unemployment rate, the hundreds of homeless boys camping out in Grant Park, the soup kitchens that were financed by gangster

Al Capone because the city was too broke to help its citizens. As I listened, my imagination filled in the details—the clattering sounds of Model T Fords, the smells of factory smoke, the taste of a ten-cent slice of pecan pie. Over time, it was as if my parents' memories became my own, memories I fashioned into a story with help from the Chicago History Museum's exhibit "Face-to-Face with the Great Depression," and Houston's National Museum of Funeral History's macabre but vivid description of a 1930s neighborhood funeral home.

**Scott**—Not far from my house, on the city's northwest side, sits the former site of Chicago State Hospital, a sorrow-filled gothic monstrosity with a long and dark history—a history I borrowed for this story. As Scott reported, inmates were abused, mistreated and abandoned at the asylum. There was, indeed, a railroad car that locals called the crazy train. And those old headlines? They came directly from historical newspapers. As for the hospital itself, it was demolished in the 1970s. But many people claim that its spirits live on. They have reported hearing the disembodied laughter of children and seeing the outlines of groaning, white-robed specters. They link this paranormal activity to the fact that a portion of the hospital's cemetery was bulldozed to make room for a strip mall—a mall that residents have nicknamed Poltergeist Square because of the city of bones lying just beneath the asphalt.

**David**—Oh, those campy 1950s science fiction movies with their flying saucers on strings and their rubber-suited monsters! They were corny, the acting in them was terrible, and I adored them as a kid. Only later did I learn that these films were deeply influenced by the 1950s preoccupation with science, space and the Communist threat. I drew on all these elements when writing this story. I also added a heaping helping of 1950s fads and fashions—rattan furniture, suburban barbecuing, pink kitchen counters and those wonderfully hokey novelty items kids bought from the backs of their comic books. Onion gum, anyone?

**Evelyn**—The setting for this story, the 1893 Chicago World's Fair, also known as the World's Columbian Exposition, must have been an astonishing event. Yes, there really was a chocolate Venus de Milo on display. Visitors really could attend a silkworm lecture at the Horticulture Building. And more than once, the moving walkway was shut down because of windy weather. As for the Palace of Fine Arts, while the secret fourth-floor gallery and the Contarini Looking Glass are figments of my imagination, the building did boast a gilded cupola, as well as thousands of world-famous paintings and sculptures by artists like Mary Cassatt and Daniel Chester French. Interestingly, the Palace of Fine Arts is the only building that still remains from the fair. Nowadays, it houses the city's Museum of Science and Industry. If you go, be sure to look up at that magnificent cupola. But beware. According to local lore, the place is haunted.

**Lily**—When I was a kid, my sister and I used to love staying up late on Friday nights to watch black-and-white reruns of *The Alfred Hitchcock Hour,* a 1960s television series about murder, mystery and the macabre. More than once we clutched each other and screamed in terror, but by far the scariest episode was the one about the monkey's paw. At the time, I didn't realize that Hitchcock was actually retelling a story that had been written in 1902 by W. W. Jacobs. I simply knew that the story was a spine-tingling mixture of maniacal Gypsy, magical object and mangled corpse rising from the grave. Scary, good fun! When my thoughts turned to writing ghost stories, I recalled this TV show, as well as the original story it was based upon, and decided to create my own version. But one thing bothered me. In neither of the earlier versions were we told what happened to the monkey's paw. In my story, I imagined it found its way into a garage sale.

**Rich**—When I was in high school, the *Chicago Tribune* ran a series of articles about supposed devil worship within the Cook County Forest Preserve. According to the newspaper, makeshift stone altars had been found, as well as bizarre symbols scratched into trees and rocks. Were teens experimenting with black magic, asked the newspaper? And if so, could their inexperienced dabbling actually summon uncontrollable and frightening phenomena? Readers responded with a resounding "Yes!" and "Yes!" Accounts of supernatural happenings poured in. Readers told of dolls and other inanimate objects suddenly possessed by evil; of getting caught in brimstone showers; of seeing hellhounds and huge black flies and other creatures that weren't found on earth. They even claimed that Mount Baldy, the largest and loveliest sand dune on the Indiana National Lakeshore, was actually a portal to Hell. Why the sudden "Satan Scare"? No one knows for sure, but just as quickly as it sprang up, it died down. No more stone altars or portals to Hell. As for Mount Baldy and the Cook County Forest Preserve, they were once again considered safe, serene parks.

**Edgar**—I first read Edgar Allan Poe's gothic tale "Berenice" when I was in sixth grade, the same year I encountered Charlotte

Perkins Gilman's "The Yellow Wallpaper." Both stories scared the socks off me. Both stories stuck with me through the years. And both stories have strong echoes in this one. So, too, does Chicago of 1870, a grim, coal-dust-covered world of robber barons and railroads, grain houses and meat packing plants. The description of Cyrus McCormick found in this story, as well as details about idyllic Prairie Avenue and the grimy city beyond, are based on English author Anthony Trollope's impressions of Chicago during his visit in 1862. As for Edgar's treatment at the hands of his own parents, sadly, it is based on truth. Back then, modern-day psychiatry did not exist. There was no help for people with mental illnesses. Those without families were simply locked up in insane asylums, while those with families— like Edgar—were often hidden away in attics and cellars, left to exist in a dark, lonely world.

**Tracy**—While the character of Aunt Viola is fictional, the story of her fiancé's murder is based on the true account of Irish gangster Dion O'Banion, bootlegger and florist to the Mob, who was shot with his arms full of roses after he'd double-crossed Al Capone. Dubbed the Murder Among the Flowers by local newspapers, it was one of the most sensational gangland hits of its day. Details of O'Banion's elaborate funeral, as reported by the *Chicago Tribune,* were so gaudily delightful I simply had to use them for Pete Winter's imaginary one. As for Capone himself, all the descriptions of his Lexington Hotel headquarters—right down to his lavender-tiled bathtub, his secret tunnels and those basement vaults where he supposedly stashed his gold—come from reports of the day. It should be noted, however, that an angry girlfriend did not cause the scars on Capone's face. These were the result of his being attacked in a Brooklyn tavern after having insulted a customer's sister. Scarface died in 1947 and was buried in Mount Carmel Cemetery in Hillside, Illinois. Every year, hundreds of visitors stream past his grave, leaving notes, cigars and, curiously, roses.

CANDACE FLEMING believes that the spookiest stories begin with the truth. The setting of this book, White Cemetery, is a real graveyard near her home in Oak Park, Illinois, not far from Chicago.

Fleming is the prolific and highly acclaimed author of numerous books for kids, including the nonfiction titles *The Lincolns: A Scrapbook Look at Abraham and Mary,* an ALA-ALSC Notable Children's Book and winner of the *Boston Globe–Horn Book* Award for Nonfiction; *The Great and Only Barnum: The Tremendous, Stupendous Life of Showman P. T. Barnum,* also an ALA-ALSC Notable Children's Book, as well as an ALA-YALSA Best Book for Young Adults; and *Amelia Lost: The Life and Disappearance of Amelia Earhart,* which *Kirkus Reviews* called a "stunning look at an equally stunning lady." In addition, Fleming is the author of the Aesop Elementary School books for middle-grade readers and the picture books *Clever Jack Takes the Cake,* a *School Library Journal* Best Book of the Year, and *Imogene's Last Stand,* which was a Junior Library Guild selection. You can visit the author at candacefleming.com.